DEADLY CULT

Deadly Cult

By the Author

Pursued

Deadly Cult

DEADLY CULT

by

Joel Gomez-Dossi

A Division of Bold Strokes Books

2013

DEADLY CULT

ISBN 13: 978-1-60282-895-7

This Trade Paperback Original Is Published By
Bold Strokes Books, Inc.

CREDITS
EDITORS: GREG HERREN AND STACIA SEAMAN
PRODUCTION DESIGN: STACIA SEAMAN
COVER DESIGN BY SHERI (GRAPHICARTIST2020@HOTMAIL.COM)

Acknowledgments

Many thanks to the staff and authors at Bold Strokes Books, publisher Len Barot, editor Greg Herren, and my husband.

Deadly Cult is dedicated to the religious and spiritual organizations that value critical thinking and open discourse.

CHAPTER ONE

Zacchaeus scanned the room to make sure he was alone. He took a small package from his pocket and meticulously tied it with hemp string. He attached a card with the name and address of the recipients written carefully on it. He put the bundle in his pocket and carried it through the compound to the Disciples' quarters.

Luckily, no one saw him walking into Raamiah's room. He bowed before the occupant, a fat and contentious-looking man who lived up to the meaning of his name: *evil from the Lord*.

"Please, Disciple, will you deliver this for me?" He held the package in front of him with trembling hands.

Raamiah took the parcel and examined it carefully. He grinned, exposing a row of brown teeth. "What'll ya give me for this favor?"

Zacchaeus didn't dare look at Raamiah any longer than necessary, and shifted his gaze to the ground. "Whatever you desire, Disciple."

"You're going to spoil me, my dear little man."

Zacchaeus untied the drawstring to Raamiah's trousers and sensed the man's grin turning into a full smile. He had to tug at the pants until they fell to the ground, exposing the sin underneath. He took the sin in his hands. It was a gnarly-looking thing. Ugly. But Zacchaeus was fulfilling his lot in life and refused to think about it. He only thought about the desperate need to get the package to Eddie Delgado, Ellen Rhodes, and Jamie Bradford.

CHAPTER TWO

Lazarus Saturday

A tray filled with dirty dishes crashed to the ground while a jazzed-up version of "Easter Bonnet" wafted through the sound system. Silverware scattered and china broke into hundreds of pieces. Debris flew everywhere. About a dozen diners looked up, shocked that the serenity of Le Chateau, New York's world-class bistro, had been shattered.

"Shit." Jamie looked around to see who had run into him, causing the mishap, but the person had disappeared. Jamie dropped to his knees and began cleaning before the floor manager could make a big deal out of the accident.

It was too late. "Monsieur Bradford," the manager bellowed across the room. A millisecond later, he was hovering over Jamie.

"Pierre, I'm sorry. But I can explain…" Jamie's voice was barely above a whisper.

"Bradford, how many times has this happened?"

The question seemed to come out of nowhere. Jamie was shocked. "Sir, it's never happened before."

Pierre arched his eyebrows and flared his nostrils. "Well, you're wrong. This has to be the third time this month alone."

"No. I've never had an accident before." Jamie wondered

if Pierre was mistaking him for the busboy he fired last week. Or the one he dismissed three weeks before that. But with all of Pierre's ranting, Jamie decided this wasn't the best time to enter a conversation. "Perhaps I can explain everything after the shift."

"No, you can't. You won't be around when the shift ends, because after you finish picking up this mess, you're going to punch out of work and leave. For good."

"I'm fired?"

"Yes, you're fired. I can't say it any clearer than that." Pierre huffed off, spouting French curses under his breath.

Jamie figured something like this would happen eventually. Pierre hated his guts and nothing Jamie could say would change his mind. *Besides, I'm a complete failure, even at bussing tables.*

To make matters worse, Jamie's husband, Eddie Delgado, was making professional leaps. He was the sous chef at Le Chateau and had even gotten Jamie his job. "It's just temporary, until you find your direction," he told him at the time. But Jamie still didn't have any plans for the future.

He clocked out and waited in the alley for Eddie to finish his shift. Several hours later, Eddie finally exited the back door. He straightened his posture and brushed the accumulated food off his checkered baggies.

"Your leg's bothering you, isn't it?" Jamie asked, sliding off the Dumpster and giving him a kiss.

"Don't be silly. I'm tired, that's all." Eddie climbed into Jamie's place and patted the empty space by his side. Jamie got back on the garbage bin and they sat for a moment, looking down the alley and into the crowded street. "I heard about what happened," Eddie said. "Pierre's a jerk, so don't let this bother you."

"But I've never had an accident before."

"I know. But trust me, it's not worth the trouble arguing with him. Besides, you'll get another job in no time."

"You think?"

Eddie nodded and gave him a tender kiss. At that moment, Pierre sashayed into the alley with two women by his side. He broke free from his entourage and walked up to Jamie. "Monsieur Bradford, I'm disappointed that you cannot understand why I terminated your employment. I thought you were more erudite than that. But *c'est la vie*, opportunities for someone with your looks and charm should come quickly. Who knows? You might get hired to carry some guy's luggage."

Pierre turned up his nose and snapped for his retinue. He weaved down the alley with them by his side.

Jamie's body tensed, but Eddie held his hand tightly. It kept him from doing anything foolish. When Pierre was down the street, Jamie said under his breath, "I ought to sue this fucking restaurant for sexual harassment."

"It's all right. We'll get by."

"But we need the money."

"I make enough for us to survive."

Eddie was right. He was bringing in a fair salary and working for one of the biggest names in the industry, Chef Bardot. Unfortunately, Bardot was also one of the biggest sleazebags in the industry. Jamie changed the subject. "I just wish we could afford to visit our families for the holiday, and now you even have to work Easter brunch."

"Jamie, your mom wanted to visit us for Easter, but you said no."

"Well, it wouldn't be right, especially when your family can't get a visa to come up from Mexico."

"Okay," Eddie said. "I understand." He took Jamie's hand.

"I don't want to hold your hand," Jamie said with a seductive smile. "I'd much rather hold something else." He grabbed Eddie.

"Stop it. You'll make me hard."

"That was the intention." Jamie ceased his antics, and they

strolled to the street in a lovers' embrace. In the city—the Village, to be precise—nobody looked twice at a gay couple engaging in public displays of affection. Practically *passé de mode*. Totally yesterday's trend.

En route to their fourth-story, two-and-a-half-room flat, they came across a guy on the street hawking stuffed animals in colorful baskets. "Cuddly Peter Cottontails, only ten bucks! All proceeds go to Easter Seals!" he barked.

Eddie reached into his pocket, pulled out a twenty, and bought two pink-colored synthetic bunnies. The "Made in China" tags were in plain view.

Jamie was aghast. "How could you do that?"

"Do what?"

He turned even sterner. "Give money to just anybody on the street! Especially now that I'm out of work."

"The guy isn't just anybody. He's from Easter Seals, for heaven's sake."

"And do you really believe that? And do you really think he's going to give that money to them?"

Eddie thought for a moment. "For the love of God, Jamie. Why wouldn't he?"

"To keep the money for himself!"

Exasperated, Jamie started walking away and heard Eddie yell, "Jamie Bradford, you are too cynical."

Jamie spun around. Eddie was struggling to catch up with him, and Jamie felt sorry for yelling. They walked the rest of the way hand in hand. At their apartment building, Eddie walked up the steps by grasping the banister. His leg must have hurt like hell, but as usual, he didn't say anything.

That stupid Mexican machismo thing, Jamie thought.

Inside the apartment, Eddie carefully set the stuffed animals on the table. He looked exhausted as he crawled on top of the pull-down bed. He didn't bother undressing. He just closed his eyes and fell asleep.

Jamie took a moment to admire Eddie's sweet face and strong physique. The post-adolescent body he had two years ago had morphed into a handsome young man. Muscular, too.

Jamie quietly took off Eddie's food-stained tennis shoes and dropped them onto the floor. He carefully unbuttoned his checkered baggies, pulling them off the legs before starting to tackle the white socks. Jamie smelled the scent of food emanating from Eddie's body, but he didn't mind. He'd gotten used to it over the past year and kind of liked it.

He lay next to his sleeping husband and lightly caressed the old wound on Eddie's leg. He'd gotten injured helping Jamie escape a murderer, but he'd never say a word about it. Barely twenty-three years old, he was too much of a man to brag about it.

Why can't I be that way? Jamie couldn't answer his own question. Instead, he continued to play with the soft, dark hair around Eddie's scar and gently leaned over to kiss it. Eddie's caramel-colored legs stirred something within Jamie, and he began giving Eddie's body light kisses.

Eddie moaned.

"Te gusta?" Jamie asked when he reached the Jockey shorts.

"Sí. Me gusta," Eddie replied.

That's all Jamie wanted to hear, and he started crying. His pent-up frustrations flowed out. Anger at not being accepted into law school and the embarrassment of having to admit he didn't quite have it all together. He was still good-looking, but he wasn't the intellectual giant he wanted to be.

Eddie put his arms around him and hugged him tightly. "None of that matters. You're kind and caring. That's enough for me."

"Well, maybe that isn't enough for me. You're a success, so you can't understand how I feel." Jamie saw the hurt well up in Eddie's eyes. "That's not what I meant. I don't know what I mean or how I feel, except I'm not happy. Certainly not being a busboy."

"Well, you're not a busboy anymore," Eddie said, a smile on his face. "Pierre gave you an opportunity."

"What opportunity?"

"A shot at discovering what you want to do with your life. Your calling."

"You sound like a Jehovah's Witness."

"Bitch," Eddie said.

Jamie gave him a devilish look. "Well, if I'm a bitch, I'm in heat because I'm horny as hell." Jamie dug a finger into the waistband of Eddie's Jockeys.

Eddie rose to the occasion. He must not have been that tired after all.

CHAPTER THREE

Palm Sunday

The next morning, Jamie woke up horny. The sight of Eddie in the kitchenette wearing a ripped T-shirt got him aroused. He struck a sexy pose and asked, "What's my cute little *hombre* doing?"

"Cracking *huevos*." Eddie didn't even look at him.

Jamie wouldn't give up. He struck another pose. "I beg your pardon?"

Eddie turned around, stared at his provocative stance, and flatly replied, "The chicken kind of eggs."

Since Eddie wasn't in the mood for playing around, Jamie decided to get dressed. He went to a pile of clothes in the corner. After picking out his favorite *Loud and Proud* T-shirt, he checked the underarms for body odor. Satisfied, he started pulling it over his head, but stopped when he heard Eddie ask, "Can you slice the avocados for me?"

He froze, like a worried kid hiding his head in a T-shirt. "You know I always mess up cutting the avocados."

"No, you don't. But if you're worried, we can always make a fancy salsa out of it."

"If you wanted guacamole, Señor Smarty Pants, why didn't

you ask for it? That I can do." He pulled the T-shirt down and his hair stood up, filled with static electricity.

"But we have to hurry. Ellen's going to be here any second."

"It's that late?" Jamie grabbed a knife and started cutting. He and Eddie had a standing appointment for brunch with Ellen every Sunday for the past year.

She made them promise they'd never miss a week. And they all agreed. It seemed the best way to continue being friends as they went on with their lives after graduating.

"Fuck," Jamie yelled when chunks of avocado fell to the floor. He grabbed a broom and started sweeping.

Eddie slid the mortar and pestle across the counter. "Why don't you start mashing?"

Before Jamie could think of a comeback, the security buzzer rang. He patted down his hair and ran to the door.

"Hurry and let me in," Ellen commanded playfully from the intercom. "I brought the bubbly."

Jamie buzzed the door unlocked and it only took a moment until she appeared at their doorway, breathless.

"Can't you guys afford a place with an elevator?"

"In the Village?" Jamie asked. "You've gotta be joking."

"Only halfway," she said, putting the champagne in the refrigerator. "But you're never gonna believe what I've got to tell you. I was doing my first-year observation rounds at the emergency room, and this guy came in overdosing on sildenafil."

"English, please?" Jamie asked.

"Sildenafil is the generic name for Viagra. This guy had an erection for over six hours!"

"So? In high school I had a constant erection. Especially in the showers at gym class."

"That's not the funny part, sweetcakes. The guy had a twelve-inch dick. Imagine the strain of keeping that thing up!"

"Twelve inches," Jamie exclaimed. "Christ, that's not a dick. That's a foot!"

When their laughter died down, Eddie asked, "So, how's your viral load?"

Jamie's stomach jumped into his throat. He always tried to stay clear of the subject when talking with Ellen. And Eddie mentioned it as casually as the weather. "Eddie, that's not something you ask."

"It's all right," Ellen said. "At the last testing, my viral load was almost undetectable."

"What does that mean?" Jamie asked.

"It means I'm doing good."

"Then you're not positive anymore?"

"I said *almost* undetectable."

He slammed his fist on the counter. "I'm so sorry."

"There's no reason to feel guilty. You didn't give me this disease."

"But you wouldn't have gotten it, except for me."

"Jamie, that's enough." Eddie barely raised his voice, but Jamie got the message and quieted down. "Ellen, you've got to excuse Jamie. He got fired from the restaurant last night."

"Oh, sweetcakes." Ellen put her arms around him, just like she had back at Stratburgh. Eddie made it a threesome and something started vibrating.

"Since I'm sure I'm not arousing either one of you," Ellen said, "someone's cell phone must be ringing."

Eddie took out the offending accessory and talked in Spanish, a mile a minute. The only thing Jamie understood was Eddie's nods and an occasional *sí*.

When Eddie swiped the phone off, he said, "That was Tito at the restaurant. The strangest thing just happened. A package was delivered."

Jamie didn't understand what the big deal was. "What's so strange about that?"

"Well, it wasn't in a box. It's wrapped into a bundle with a piece of cloth."

"Okay, maybe that's a little different, but not earth-shattering."

"And it was addressed to all three of us. Me, you, and Ellen, too."

"Okay, that is unusual."

They didn't finish making brunch. They headed out the door, straight for Le Chateau.

CHAPTER FOUR

Bounding down the apartment stairs, Jamie was surprised that Eddie ran as quickly as he and Ellen did. But once outside, their pace came to an abrupt halt. Sunday services had let out at the church down the block. Parishioners filled the street singing "Hosanna" and carrying palm fronds fashioned into crosses.

Jamie turned to find an alternative route, but a Sunday school child approached. She gave him her cross and said, "We're celebrating. Jesus comes back next Sunday!"

Before he could say thank you, a man ran up to the girl. He glanced at Jamie and then glared at his *Loud and Proud* T-shirt with disgust written on his face. "Gretchen, how many times have I told you not to talk with strangers?" He took the little girl by her shoulders and whisked her away. But soon that family was replaced with other parishioners blocking the street. They were still singing, still waving their palm branches.

Jamie felt like he was in another world. "What is this?"

"It's Palm Sunday," Eddie replied. "Jesus rode into Jerusalem on a donkey and people laid palm branches on his path."

"Yeah," Jamie said. "I remember it from Sunday school." He dropped the girl's branch and barreled on, glancing back to make sure Ellen and Eddie were following.

It didn't take long for them to get to the restaurant. Inside, the halogen work lights were so bright they washed out every color in the room. Chairs were stacked on tables and Tito wielded a mop, making the tiled floor sparkle.

"*Gracias,*" Tito said. Then he continued in English, studiously pausing before each word. "Thank you for rushing." Tito's voice quivered and he looked horror-struck.

"Why?" Eddie asked.

"I was scared without…without…"

"You were scared shitless?" Eddie suggested.

"*Sí.* No shit. The man was creepy." Tito held out a linen package and Eddic took it. He untied the bundle, holding the contents out so everyone could see. It was a papyrus-like piece of paper, rolled up and stuck inside a school ring.

A Stratburgh University school ring.

Eddie slipped out the paper and handed the ring to Jamie, who looked inside the band for an inscription. There was none.

Eddie read the message and threw the paper onto the bar. "It doesn't make any sense."

"But what did it say?" Ellen asked.

Eddie held up the paper and began reading. "'Dear friends: To every thing there is a season, and a time to every purpose under heaven…A time to love, and a time to hate; a time of war, and a time of peace. Please, fulfill your purpose.'"

"That is weird," Jamie said. "Is it signed?"

"No. It ends with 'The Brethren, One Rhodes Plaza, Boston.' Like I told you, none of it makes any sense."

"One thing does, sort of," Ellen argued. "One Rhodes Plaza is a street address. But if I remember, the Massachusetts office isn't in Boston. It's in one of the 'burbs."

Jamie started putting the pieces together. "Could the Brethren be a tenant in the Rhodes building?"

"I doubt it," Ellen said. "Daddy doesn't lease out his empty offices. Besides, I've never heard of the Brethren. Have you?"

"Hang on." Jamie got out his smartphone and did a web search. The results flashed seconds later. "The Brethren doesn't have their own website, but a lot of other people have written about them."

"What do they say?" Ellen asked.

"Well, according to one site about alternative Christian denominations, the Brethren adheres to a strict interpretation of the Bible. And in order to avoid interacting with the world, they've sequestered themselves in the Adirondack Mountains."

"They sound like a bunch of nut cases to me," Eddie said.

Jamie shrugged. "Let's see what their wiki page has to say." He clicked another link. "Get a load of this. 'Many organizations, including the American Council of Conservative Christians, believe the Brethren to be a cult and not a bona fide religion.'"

"See?" Eddie pointed to the piece of papyrus. "It's all a sick joke."

Ellen nodded, but Jamie didn't agree. "This isn't a joke. Someone's sending us a message!"

"How can you think that?" Eddie asked. "If this is a message, it's from a highly dysfunctional person."

"Possibly. But it's more than a message. It's a plea." Jamie picked up the message and read it again. "The note came inside a Stratburgh University class ring, so there's got to be a connection. All of us graduated from Stratburgh. Do you think this guy sent us his own class ring?"

"No. We don't know who owns the ring," Ellen told him.

Eddie agreed. "Remember, there isn't an inscription. Even if it was his ring, we don't know who he is."

"Okay. But how did he know that we could be reached at Le Chateau?"

"That's public knowledge," Eddie said. "Remember the advertisements Chef Bardot placed in those food and travel magazines? In the ad's picture, I was standing right behind him."

How could Jamie forget? The ad was even in *Bon Appétit*.

"Eddie's right," Ellen said. "The sender could have seen the ad anywhere. And remember, *he* could be a *she*."

Jamie held up the ring. "Look at the size of this. This is a guy's ring. And even if Eddie's workplace was common knowledge, how did the sender know about you and me?" Ellen didn't answer, so he continued. "Maybe we can find a clue in the address card. Do you recognize the handwriting?" He handed the card to Ellen.

"Why should I recognize the handwriting?" Ellen looked at it, anyway. Then she handed it back. "Nope. Don't recognize it. It's pretty sloppy handwriting, though."

Jamie's eyes grew wide. He grabbed the card and compared it with the writing on the message. He lightly touched each letter. "Whoever wrote this used a fountain pen. Or even a quill. Look at the lettering. The strokes are fat and the ink bleeds all over the paper."

Eddie looked at the writing. "Okay. The sender didn't use a ballpoint pen. What about it?"

"I'm thinking this guy got indoctrinated by the Brethren, and now he's begging us to do something. Maybe he wants some kind of intervention."

"You're imagining things," Eddie cried. "It's just a crazy letter. And it's one week before Easter, Jamie. I'm in charge of the restaurant's brunch, I can't go on a wild goose chase."

Jamie stopped and looked at Eddie. "I'm not asking you to go with me. But it can't hurt to investigate. It's not like I have a job anymore. Besides, this will be easy. Ellen goes to Boston to find the Rhodes Petroleum connection while I go to the Brethren's headquarters in the Adirondacks. If we leave tomorrow, I bet we'd be home in about a week. Are you up for it, Ellen?"

"Sure. I have midterm break next week."

"Perfect. Then you and I will do this." Jamie looked over at his husband. "Sure you don't want to come with?"

"I already told you, I've got to work. And by the way, I'm fine being alone on Easter." Eddie walked out of the restaurant.

Embarrassed, Jamie looked over at Ellen and shrugged.

CHAPTER FIVE

Jamie walked with Ellen to his apartment without saying a word. When they got inside, Eddie wasn't there, but that didn't surprise Jamie. He'd never seen Eddie get so angry before, or so irrational. Eddie always seemed to understand him and never got mad.

Until now.

Jamie's emotions were a mess, but sitting on the edge of the pull-down, he pretended not to care. He told Ellen, "I guess Eddie just doesn't understand why this is so important."

Ellen sat next him. "Maybe I don't understand, either. After all, the letter could be a joke."

"It wasn't a joke, Ellen. Somebody needs our help," he said. "And it's obvious that person thinks we're the only ones who can help him. And if Eddie refuses to come along, we'll just do it by ourselves."

"Okay," Ellen said. "But may I ask a question?"

He nodded.

"Why didn't that person sign the letter? If he wanted help, he could get it a lot faster if we knew who he was."

Jamie didn't have an answer but was too embarrassed to admit it. "Maybe he couldn't."

"Because he was afraid?"

"Yeah, that's possible."

"What would he be afraid of, Jamie?"

He thought a moment, but could only answer with "Maybe he just didn't want to be identified. There could be lots of reasons why he's afraid."

"Then why did he contact us and not someone better qualified to help?"

"I don't have the answers, Ellen. All I know is this is something I have to do. Not only for whoever wrote the note, but for me."

"For you, sweetcakes? Why is this so important for you?"

He didn't want to answer that question, so his eyes strayed from Ellen. "You and Eddie wouldn't understand."

"What wouldn't we understand?"

"What it's like not to be successful."

Ellen took his hand, and he closed his eyes.

❖

Later that evening, after Ellen left, Eddie finally came home. Jamie was already tucked inside the lumpy bed, but he was far from asleep. "How was work, sweetie?"

Eddie didn't say anything, didn't even look at him. Eddie started getting undressed as if he were alone.

Jamie pretended everything was normal. "I bet that it wasn't very busy because everyone is going out for Easter brunch instead."

"Maybe," Eddie mumbled.

"Personally, I don't understand Easter's importance. I mean, compared to Christmas. You get presents at Christmas. Easter is only about candy."

"Jamie, please. Be quiet."

He looked away. "I'm sorry."

"You never understand my needs."

"But I try to."

"Then why do you continue blasting through every time we have a disagreement?"

"Blasting through?"

"Yes, continuing to talk as if my feelings aren't important enough to consider."

"Eddie, I'm sorry. But I don't know what you're feeling anymore because you never tell me your feelings."

"Okay," Eddie said. "My job at Le Chateau is important to me. I don't want to do anything to jeopardize it."

"You're not going to lose your job. You're too talented."

"No. There are hundreds of sous chefs out there just as qualified as I am. What keeps me employed is that I work harder and longer than they do. And now you want me to take time off to go on this mission, which is like hunting armadillos."

"What?" Jamie couldn't understand Eddie at all.

"Growing up in Laredo, all the hyper-straight jocks bragged about going armadillo hunting."

"Okay. But why would anybody hunt armadillos?"

"That's my point," Eddie said. "Nobody eats armadillos anymore. And hunting them isn't a sport. They shoot them as a joke. Something to brag about."

"Do you think I need something to brag about?"

"That's not what I said."

"But that's what you meant, so let's just forget this conversation ever happened, okay?"

Eddie began massaging Jamie's shoulders "We can't."

"Why not?" Jamie asked, relaxing his shoulders.

Eddie gave him a light kiss on the forehead. "Because I asked for time off. I know how important this is to you."

"Really?"

"Yeah. Do you think I'd let you go out in the middle of the wilderness by yourself? Not on your life."

Eddie leaned over and kissed Jamie. It wasn't a passionate kiss, but it was filled with love and understanding. It comforted Jamie. "Thank you, Eddie."

"It's okay. I got six days off, but Bardot wasn't happy about it. I have to be back at the restaurant for Easter brunch. Or else."

Jamie nodded. "I understand. So, when do we leave?"

Eddie smiled. "As soon as we can rent a car."

CHAPTER SIX

Holy Monday

Ellen didn't need to rent a car. When she got the go-ahead from Jamie, she threw clothes and her meds into a backpack and headed for the parking garage. She was in her Porsche Speedster and on the interstate before the sun came out. Being awake at such an ungodly hour, her vision was blurry. But she didn't care. *At least I'll be in Boston by nine.*

When she reached New Haven, she connected the Speedster's Bluetooth to her cell phone. She wanted to talk with her father and figured the best way to track him down would be through his secretary. She got voicemail, so she tried Rosalita, the maid at her father's estate in Westchester. Rosalita said that her father was in Boston for a series of big meetings.

Talk about luck! Ellen shifted into overdrive. She didn't want to miss an opportunity to be with her father.

❖

Jamie and Eddie were the first in line when the Rent-A-Junker office opened. Eddie had to haggle with the guy to get a decent price, but when they got to the car, Jamie wondered if they were still paying too much. Calling it a piece of junk was being kind. It was two-toned, green and rust. But he knew renting a car beat owning one and having to pay for insurance, maintenance, and renting a parking space.

They threw their duffel bags into the trunk and Eddie drove straight to the Northway. By the time they got to the Catskill Mountains, the fog had turned to a light but constant rain. Jamie watched the scenery zip by. He couldn't help but remember two years ago and their experience with Stephen Antonelli. He glanced at Eddie, who appeared to be concentrating on the road. Jamie figured Eddie had to be thinking about Antonelli, too. After all, Antonelli was the one who had messed up his leg.

Jamie wanted that part of their lives to fade away, like a bad dream. He knew, however, that it hadn't been a nightmare. It was real.

And Antonelli would always be in their memories, lurking.

They drove another hundred miles, and the rain turned into icy sleet. "Jesus, just what we need," Jamie said. "By the time we reach the Adirondacks, it's going to be snowing."

"Well, sit back and relax," Eddie told him. "We've got at least another hundred and fifty miles to go."

"That far?" Jamie looked at the GPS on his cell phone. Then he looked out the window and saw the cars ahead of them slow down because of the weather. Some drivers were on the side of the road, waiting for the sleet to clear. "Do you want to pull over and wait for the salt trucks?" he asked.

"Maybe," Eddie said. "Of course, once they come out, it'll just take longer because we won't be able to get around them."

"Well, call me a dick if you want, but I say let's take our chances and try to pull through it."

"Okay, Jamie, you're a dick. But that's one of your best body parts." Eddie smiled and continued on.

Chapter Seven

Massachusetts avoided New York's bad weather, but Ellen got waylaid trying to get to her father nonetheless. She got stuck in traffic because one of the *We Are the 99%* protests set up camp in the Boston suburb of Dedham, right in front of the Rhodes Petroleum Building. Annoyed at the delay, she drummed her fingers on the steering wheel. It wasn't the protest against Rhodes Petroleum that bothered her. It was a particular demonstrator carrying an effigy of her father. He screamed that Rhodes was a shyster.

She felt the flush of shame rise in her. *But if Daddy deserves criticism for his business behavior, don't I warrant disapproval too? He supports me, after all.*

She slouched into the driver's seat and drove past the demonstration, parking in the public garage. Afraid the protestors might hassle her for entering the Rhodes building, she hustled through the underground tunnel instead.

Entering the lobby's interior made her feel unwelcome. About a dozen video cameras hung on the walls, their red lights flashing. A security guard, most likely an off-duty police officer, checked visitors' IDs. Ellen didn't see many visitors, though. Only a couple of businesspeople carrying briefcases. They whispered to each other in the corner.

Ellen signed in, showing her driver's license to the rent-a-cop. "I'm here to see my father, Elden Rhodes."

The woman peeked at the license. "And your name is Ellen?"

"Yeah. It is." She gave the officer a friendly smile.

"One moment, please." The rent-a-cop got on the phone, covering her mouth so Ellen couldn't hear what was being said. Pretty strange behavior, Ellen thought. But she often encountered bizarre conduct when visiting her father at one of his buildings. She figured most employees got nervous at having to deal with the owner's daughter.

The security guard hung up the phone and said, "It shouldn't be long now, miss."

Seconds later, a man in a gray suit with a U.S. flag on his lapel appeared out of nowhere. Ellen was surprised to see a tiny Bluetooth headset stuck in his ear.

Ultra high-tech. The kind of hardware you'd expect the CIA to have. This guy's definitely not a junior exec.

"My name is Johnston," he said, walking up to them. "What seems to be the problem?"

Ellen spoke first. "I didn't think there was a problem."

The guard said, "She says she's Elden Rhodes's daughter."

Johnston gave Ellen a once-over, and she had a gnawing feeling something was amiss. She just couldn't put her finger on what it was. "Is Mr. Rhodes expecting you?" he asked.

"No. I'm afraid he isn't," she answered respectfully. "I was hoping to surprise him."

"Well, I talked with the operations manager just this morning. He said Mr. Rhodes wasn't expecting any visitors today."

Ellen shrugged. "As I said, I came here to surprise him. Look, call Marianne, my father's executive secretary. She'll vouch for me."

He gave her another hard look, and her gnawing feeling grew stronger. He said, "I'm afraid Mr. Rhodes's staff isn't available at this time."

"Well, I have more IDs, if you need them." Ellen started searching her backpack, digging through clothes and meds.

Then a light flashed at the security guard's desk. At the side of the lobby, an unmarked door opened and two dark-suited men came through. They had the same CIA intercom pieces stuck in their ears as Johnston did.

The men stopped in unison and the two businesspeople waiting in the lobby walked over to them. The four stood at attention and Ellen realized they were part of a security patrol.

Johnston looked around nervously and yelled into his Bluetooth. "Code red. Repeat, code red." The security patrol put their hands at their hips, in a battlelike stance, revealing their handguns. Ellen quickly surveyed the area to figure out what was happening. She didn't see much. Only a distinguished-looking gentleman coming through the door.

Johnston said "shit," and tried to grab Ellen's backpack from her, but she held on to it tightly. Straining her neck, she tried to get a better look at the man everyone was so excited about. He wore a topcoat and hat with a few wisps of white hair exposed.

She immediately recognized the gentleman and yelled, "Daddy."

The security patrol barricaded Ellen's father and escorted him back through the door. Johnston, meanwhile, gave Ellen's arm a karate chop. She dropped the backpack and he picked it up, tossing it to the rent-a-cop. He pulled her arms behind her back and cuffed her in one swift move.

Then he escorted her down another set of stairs and pushed her through a long hallway, then into a corner of a fallout shelter. She landed with a terrible crash.

Johnston yelled, "Just who are you really?"

Between the gasps, she said, "I told you. I'm Ellen Rhodes. Elden Rhodes's daughter."

"Yeah. And I'm the Prince of Persia."

She wasn't going to let him get the better of her. "Good to meet you, your highness."

He backed up a couple of steps and swung his leg backward to kick her. She recoiled in fear.

The doors to the shelter opened and the words "What the hell is going on here?" flew from the entrance. It came from Ellen's father.

Everyone froze and looked over at him.

Ellen cried, "Daddy!" He ran to her side and she hugged him without reserve.

"Sweet Pea! Are you hurt?" Usually Ellen hated it when he called her Sweet Pea, but not today. Right now, she was happy to hear anything from him.

"Mr. Rhodes." Johnston took several steps back and got out the key to the restraints. Her father grabbed them from his hands and unlocked the cuffs himself. "Ellen, you showed them your license when they asked for it, didn't you?"

"Of course, Daddy."

Johnston interrupted, "Sir, in our defense, IDs can be forged."

"An official state license with a holographic image? Did you even look at it?"

"The officer at the desk did, sir."

"But that's not you, is it?"

Johnston looked him square in the eyes. "I was just following protocol."

"I don't care. Tell your superiors at Tactical Protective Services that I'm ending my contract with them. I can get better security from the guards at a zoo. I want you and your detail to pack up and leave."

"You know, sir, it will take months for you to contract another security unit."

"You heard me. Get out of here."

And that was that. Everyone left, and Ellen was with her father, for the first time in a very long time.

"Daddy, was that a wise thing to do? Don't you need your security?"

"Yes, and we'll contract a new vendor in good time. But right now my priority is to be with you."

She nearly hyperventilated with happiness, until her father said, "And we'll be together right after my meeting. You understand, don't you, Sweet Pea?"

She said, "Of course, Daddy."

CHAPTER EIGHT

B y the time Jamie and Eddie reached the Adirondacks, the sleet had morphed into flurries, making travel even slower. Eddie pulled into a decrepit gas station. He filled the tank while Jamie went inside to ask for directions.

An old man sat by the cash register, reading a copy of *The Penny Saver*. Jamie handed him a couple of twenties for the gas. The man pocketed it without looking away from his paper.

"Excuse me," Jamie said. "I'm looking for a church around here. They go by the name of the Brethren. Heard of them?"

"Yeah, I heard of 'em." The man chortled. His cigarette didn't move, like it was stuck to his lower lip. The cigarette's long ash dangled at the end, like it was stuck there by magic.

"I was wondering if you could give me directions."

"Yeah, if I felt like it." The man held out his hand, rubbing his index and middle fingers with his thumb.

So it's going to be that way, Jamie thought. He dug into his pocket and handed the man a twenty. "Will this motivate you?"

"It might." The attendant pocketed the twenty and tore off a page from his *Penny Saver*. He licked the point of a stubby pencil without disturbing the cigarette and began drawing a map on the paper. When he finished, he pushed it to the edge of the counter.

"Thanks." Jamie looked at it, then handed it back. "But could you put the names of the roads on it, too?"

"Nope. Can't do that," the man said.

"Why not?

"'Cause there ain't no names. Just roads." He stuffed the map into Jamie's pocket.

"Ah, I understand." Jamie gave the man another twenty.

"Thank you for your generosity," he said, taking the money. "But there still ain't no names."

"Well, since that's the case." Jamie snatched back the bill.

"Okay, okay. I'll see what I can do." The attendant took the money and gently tugged the map out of Jamie's pocket. The ash on his cigarette still hung on.

Jamie watched as the man drew pictures and symbols describing the roads. "But you'll never be able to travel on most of them," he said. "Not with that jalopy of yours. It'll be too rough and rocky. Or muddy." He finished his artwork and held it up.

"I appreciate the warning," Jamie said.

"Well, if you get stuck, give me a call. I got a tow truck. Real reasonable rates." The ash on his cigarette finally fell off, landing on his shirt.

Jamie walked outside and Eddie was waiting for him. "Did you get directions?" Eddie asked when he got into car.

"Yeah, if it'll do any good."

Jamie pointed north and Eddie put the rental into gear.

❖

Surprisingly, the attendant's directions were pretty accurate. So was his description of the roads. They were rutted and muddy.

Halfway there, they got stuck and couldn't budge the car an inch. "So, what do we do now?" Eddie asked. "Call that guy and get a tow?"

"Not on your life," Jamie said. "We start walking."

"And leave the car here? The police will come by and tow it."

"Eddie, look at this road. Nobody uses it. It'll be months before anyone finds this car."

"Unless someone from the Brethren comes by."

"We'll camouflage it, then. It'll be safe."

"You sure?"

"Almost positive."

"Just almost?"

Jamie smiled and said, "Okay. I'm absolutely almost positive."

They got out of the car and scavenged around until they had enough greenery to cover it. When they finished, Jamie said, "Just one more thing to do." He took out his driver's license and put it into an envelope.

"Why are you doing that?" Eddie asked.

"When we get inside the Brethren and somebody there sees our licenses, they'll know we live together. They won't believe we're just roommates. They may be conservative, but they're not dumb." He held the envelope in front of Eddie.

"I guess you're right." Eddie took the envelope and stuck in his license, too. Just as he was about to seal the flap, Jamie stopped him.

"We forgot one thing." He took off his wedding ring and put it into the envelope.

"Our rings?"

Jamie gave him a kiss. "Sweetie, forgive me, but we have to." He knew it wouldn't be worthy recompense if they lost their wedding bands, but he was afraid they'd lose much more if the Brethren figured out their relationship.

Eddie reluctantly took off his ring and put it in the envelope. "I suppose this means we'll have to go back into the closet."

"Yeah," Jamie said. He was apprehensive because he knew acting straight would be hard. He took the envelope anyway and placed it into the glove box. "Are you ready to go on another adventure, my secret husband?"

Eddie grinned and said, *"Si."*

They got out and trudged through the mud. After a quarter mile, Jamie realized Eddie's leg must have started hurting again. His strides became shorter, his limp more pronounced, and he held on to tree branches for support. Eddie asked, "What will we tell the Brethren when we get there?"

That was an easy question for Jamie. "We'll tell them we're spiritual pilgrims, seeking enlightenment."

"Sounds like bull to me."

"They'll eat it up, trust me."

❖

When they reached the end of the road, their map indicated it was the Brethren's compound. But there weren't any clues that it was a church—there were no steeples or statues of saints. A No Trespassing sign hung from the electronically controlled steel gate, and so did a sign that read *Danger, electrified fence.* Branching from each side of the gate was a twenty-foot-tall chain-link fence that sprawled for miles.

"Looks like an army base," Eddie exclaimed. "Or a prison."

Jamie had to agree. "Onward Christian Soldiers," he said, but he was thinking, *Who are they trying to keep out? Or keep in?* He didn't have time to formulate an answer, though. He heard something in the distance. "Did you hear that?" he asked Eddie.

"Hear what?"

There was a crunch in the snow. Jamie looked into Eddie's eyes and saw them grow bigger. The crunches got louder and nearer. Jamie paused, then jumped up and down, waving his arms like he was a castaway on a deserted island. "We're here! We're over here!" he yelled. It must have looked like he lost his marbles.

From the other side of the gate, an obese, dirty man stumbled out of the bushes. He was dressed like an Amish elder. He wore simple, linen clothes that were disheveled. And he looked ornery. Very ornery.

"Who are you and what are you doing here?"

"We're two lost souls, searching for the light of God," Jamie replied.

"What the…"

Jamie gave Eddie a jab in the ribs for him to give it try. "We've come to the Brethren to find the way, the truth, and the life."

"Yeah, as if I believe that," the man said, moving in closer the gate. "Okay, who are you? Really. Your names."

"My name is Eddie. And this is my husb—my friend, Jamie."

"Really?" The cantankerous man started laughing. His head thrashed up and down, exposing a mouth filled with brown teeth. He regained control and pulled out a revolver. "You boys tell a good story, but it's just that. A story. You're not seeking enlightenment."

"Yes, we are," Jamie said. "I swear to God."

"We don't swear here, so shut up," the man yelled back. "And even if I did believe you, do you think the Brethren would accept anyone off the street?"

Neither answered.

The man shook his gun again. "Well, do you?"

"No, sir," Jamie replied.

"You're damn right, we wouldn't. Most people aren't worthy of belonging to the Brethren."

"Aren't we supposed to love our neighbors?" Jamie asked.

The fat man raised his gun to Jamie's face. "I'll tell you what I love. My weapon. So I suggest you get your scrawny ass out of here before I use it for target practice."

"All right. All right." Jamie held his arms above his head. He and Eddie slowly backed up the road about a hundred feet. At the first clearing, Jamie steered Eddie into the woods, opposite of the way they arrived, and they started running as fast as they could.

They came upon a strange-looking building with only three walls. "What the heck is this?" Eddie asked.

"It's a lean-to," Jamie told him. Growing up in Wisconsin, he'd seen lots of them. Not much to see, though. Basically a roof with a single slope, three walls, and a large open space where the fourth wall should be. Eddie lay on the bench inside, and Jamie sat next to him. He gently rubbed Eddie's leg.

After a moment of contented silence, Jamie finally said, "It's too suspicious."

"What is?"

"Well, something isn't right about a religion turning away potential converts. It only makes me more determined to find out what the hell they're hiding."

There wasn't an answer, so he looked down at Eddie. He was asleep.

CHAPTER NINE

Zacchaeus sat in his room. A hallway, really. His eyes were heavy and he looked forward to resting on his mat for a few hours. He had cooked the Disciples' supper, wild turkey with root vegetables. Then he finished their laundry and did as much of their mending as he possibly could. There were so many to be cared for, and he was so weary.

He recited a hymn that gave him comfort. *Work is sweet, for God has blest honest work with quiet rest.* But he didn't have a chance to finish the song, or to relax. Disciple Raamiah burst in.

"My dear little Zacchaeus," he said, picking leftover turkey from his teeth. "You'll never guess who I ran into today."

"Who, Disciple Raamiah?" He didn't want to talk with him, but didn't dare rebuke him, either.

"Your boyfriends. That Eddie Delgado and Jamie Bradford. They came to the gates, wanting to get in. I don't know where their girlfriend was, though."

Zacchaeus's hands started shaking. "I don't know what you're talking about."

"Oh, it's a pity you have such a short memory." Raamiah reached down, grabbed Zacchaeus's crotch, and squeezed. "Lucky for us, other things aren't so limited."

Zacchaeus stood still as Raamiah burrowed his face into his neck. He smelled Raamiah's bad breath and his body tensed. "I already paid you for that favor," he said, his voice as unstable as his hands.

"But there are many more favors that payment is still owed for."

"We made no other deals."

"We may not have explicitly agreed upon them, but we made them. And I've lived up to my part of the bargain."

"What did you do?"

"Well, I sent your boyfriends away, for instance."

"You did?"

"Yeah. I sent them packing. Now you won't get in trouble."

"Trouble for what?" He asked the question, but he already knew the answer. Contact with the outside was forbidden, especially for someone as lowly as he was.

Raamiah just laughed. "Well, I can list the reasons now. Or should I save us both some time? After all, you know what I want."

Raamiah was right. He knew what Raamiah wanted. He took Raamiah's hand, led him to a secluded part of the quarters, and let him take it.

CHAPTER TEN

Ellen drank hot chocolate while she waited in Marianne's office for her father. She had lost count of how many cups she had consumed, she'd been there so long. When he finally stopped by, they went into his office to talk.

She took a comfortable guest chair and her father planted himself behind his large mahogany desk. "So why did you come up?"

He always got down to business. She couldn't remember him ever being concerned about her personal life, school and friends, that kind of thing. Business was as close to personal as he ever got.

She started to answer him, but never got the chance. Marianne buzzed him on the intercom. "Mr. Rhodes, the senior senator from Texas is on the phone for you. He says it's urgent."

"I could care less what that S.O.B. says. I contribute enough to his Super PACS. If he wants to speak to me, he can make an appointment."

"Yes, Mr. Rhodes." He was about to disconnect when Marianne spoke again. "One more thing, sir. May I assign someone to contact potential security firms?"

"Does this have to be done now?" He looked at Ellen, and she smiled back politely.

Marianne continued, "You do have some public appearances coming up."

"With Bible thumpers. I think we'll get by."

"Of course, Mr. Rhodes."

He disconnected the intercom, then his telephone rang. He looked at the caller ID and said, "This is from my lawyer on the private line. Mind if I take it?"

It would be useless to say no, so she acquiesced with a shrug. He turned on his speakerphone and relaxed in his chair. "Yeah, Harry. What's up?"

Harry's voice sprang from the speaker. "Glad I was able to catch you, Mr. Rhodes. This is of vital importance."

"I'm with my daughter, Harry. Can we do this another time?"

"But it's about the Minnesota state representative, Mr. Rhodes. She's mad that you didn't donate to her Morality Initiative. She's threatening to retaliate."

"Does she have the power?"

"I doubt it."

"Then I'll talk with you about it later." He turned his phone off and said, "Sorry, Sweet Pea."

"That's okay, Daddy. I'm the one who's intruding." She wished she wasn't an intrusion in her father's life, but doubted that would ever change.

"So, why did you travel all this way to see me?" He checked his watch and looked antsy. Ellen knew she'd better speak up or she'd lose this chance.

"Well, it's actually about Rhodes Petroleum."

His face got serious. "What about it?"

"You remember Jamie and Eddie, don't you?"

"Who?"

"My friends from Stratburgh University."

"Sorry, I don't remember them."

Her chest tightened, but she continued, "They're the guys who rescued me when I was kidnapped two years ago."

"Oh, the gay ones. Now I remember. I've never met them, have I?"

"No, Daddy."

"Didn't think so."

She took a breath to calm down. "We got this crazy package. There was a message inside. It had the address to this particular office of Rhodes Petroleum on it, along with the name of a cult based in New York. The Brethren. I'm wondering if there could be a link between the two."

Her father paused a moment, then shook his head. "Sorry."

"But there has to be something that ties them together, or why would somebody send a message like that?"

"Because the world is filled with crazies, Ellen."

There he goes again, she thought. "No, I don't agree with you, Daddy. There's a reason for the things people do."

Her forcefulness surprised her, and even her father's face showed some shock. He rephrased his statement. "Okay. Then it's their reasons that are crazy." He walked over to the window and opened the blinds. He pointed at the demonstrators on the sidewalk. "Look at them. They're protesting because I make money by producing gasoline. But who consumes that fuel? They do. And they continue to drive their gas-guzzlers while complaining about the cost of fuel."

Ellen dug her nails into her fingertips. "Daddy, this isn't what I want to talk with you about."

"I'm sorry," he said. "Then what do you want from me?"

She didn't have to think about her request. "Two of your employees to help me find a connection."

"But you don't get them full-time. I'll give you ten hours total for both of them. Who do you want?"

"First, one of your private investigators. He can access records that I can't get."

"Done. Who next?"

"I'll also need someone to guide me around the company. With the information the PI can get me, plus a little time, I know I can find the link I'm looking for."

"I can do that, too. See? All you had to do is ask." He turned on his intercom. "Marianne, get me Christian Donahue. I need him to find a new security firm. And I also have another job he might enjoy."

He grinned at Ellen and clicked the intercom off. "Christian is my newest junior executive, but he has a wealth of knowledge about the company. If he can't help you, no one can."

It didn't take long before there was a knock at the door and it opened. A good-looking man entered. He had muscular, chiseled features and dark, wavy hair. "I'm Christian Donahue," he said. "You sent for me, Mr. Rhodes?"

Ellen's heart raced. If this guy was half as smart as he was handsome, she'd enjoy her stay in Boston.

CHAPTER ELEVEN

Jamie guessed it was late in the afternoon because the sun was about to set. He would have checked the time on his cell phone, but it was in his backpack. Reaching for it would have wakened Eddie. But Eddie woke anyway, sitting up with a jolt. "Jamie, do you have a plan yet?"

Jamie looked at him and said, "Not since the last time you asked."

"When was that?"

"About ten minutes ago."

"Do you know when you'll come up with a plan?"

"No, but I'll tell you when I have one."

"I'm confused. You'll tell me when you come up with a plan, or when you come up with a time estimate for a plan?"

"Either one. Go back to sleep, Eddie."

"I love you, too, Jamie." He closed his eyes again.

Jamie caressed his drowsy husband's cheek and wondered how they could gain access to the Brethren now that they'd been seen and chased away. And even if they did get in, what were they supposed to discover? Maybe Ellen and Eddie were right. Maybe the package was a big fat joke.

He looked into the horizon. The sun peeked out of the clouds and it felt a bit warmer. More importantly, the skies began to clear. *Thank God for spring, even in the Adirondacks.*

He heard something in the distance that sounded like car engines. But it couldn't have been just one engine. The sound was so loud it had to be an army brigade.

He looked down the hill and saw a battalion of SUVs climbing upward. These weren't ordinary vehicles, though. These had to be Hummers on steroids because they cleared the rocks, mud, and gunk with ease.

He woke Eddie, and they watched the brigade move closer.

"Think they're from the Brethren?" Jamie asked.

Eddie nodded.

"Then we'd better hide. Don't want them seeing us as they drive by."

They grabbed their duffel bags and hid in the nearby bushes. But the brigade didn't drive by. Moments later, the lead vehicle stopped right in front of the lean-to. The rest of the SUVs—all five of them—stopped in a queue.

The lead driver climbed out and posed like an army general. They were so close Jamie could almost smell him. He heard the driver bark to the other drivers, "All right, we've got to take an unplanned break."

The driver of the second SUV practically fell out of his vehicle getting out. He ran over to the commander. "But, Brother Gideon, we're so close to the compound."

Gideon scowled. He opened the door to his SUV and a frail teenager got out. The kid had to be about eighteen. "I'm sorry," the kid said with a nasal voice. He sounded almost comical.

Gideon turned to his subordinate and imitated the sinus-funneled kid. "He didn't take a leak the last time we fueled up. The last few miles, he fidgeted so much, I got worried he'd pee all over our leather seats."

The two men laughed while the teen, looking red with shame, went to the bushes. He started to unzip his pants and looked right in Jamie's direction. Jamie and Eddie froze in a squatting position. Jamie prayed the kid wouldn't notice them. It was a lost cause, though, and Jamie just smiled at him. Thankfully, the shocked teenager was just as frightened as Jamie. He zipped up his pants and turned his attention to a pinecone in front of him. But most importantly, he didn't give them away.

Jamie, relieved, turned his attention to the drivers. The subordinate got serious and asked Brother Gideon, "Should we let all the new Faithfuls take a break?"

Gideon threw up his hands. "Why the hell not? It's not like we can make up any time now. But only to piss, mind you. They'll have to wait until we reach HQ for anything else."

The subordinate pulled out his walkie-talkie and addressed all the SUVs. There must have been a radio communications system because his voice boomed through speakers on top of each vehicle. "Time for a rest stop, everyone. Men should use the right side of the lean-to. The women who have to go should use the opposite side. Sister Naomi will distribute the wet naps when you return."

The passengers unloaded, and Jamie was shocked. They held lots of new Faithfuls. There were twelve to fifteen for each vehicle—men and women of varying in sizes, shapes, and ethnicities. There was only one defining attribute. Judging by their clothing, they were all well-off.

Not just financially comfortable, but very wealthy.

Jamie looked at the throng of people and whispered, "Holy shit. There have to be seventy-five of them."

"At least," Eddie whispered back.

Jamie gleamed. He had an idea. "Do you think they'd notice a couple more?"

Eddie grinned and said, "Probably not."

Hidden by all the Faithfuls trudging into the woods, Jamie stood up and asked the shy teen, "Mind if we join you?"

He shook his head, and Jamie and Eddie joined the crowd. When everyone was finished, they were herded back to the vehicles. Jamie nodded thanks to the kid and followed the crowd.

He and Eddie found an older gentleman to accompany.

"Grandpa Swanson," he introduced himself. "Only I don't have any grandchildren. Or I might as well not have any. They only loved me for my money anyway."

When they approached the SUV, Grandpa Swanson said, with his eyes twinkling, "But I showed my kids that I'm the boss. I changed my will. The Brethren gets everything now. My family, the ungrateful bastards, will be left without a cent."

Jamie said, "Good for you, Grandpa." He and Eddie boarded the SUV behind the elderly man.

"Aren't you boys getting on the wrong bus?" Grandpa Swanson asked. "You weren't on this one before."

"Of course we were," Jamie told him. "You told us all about your ungrateful children. Don't you remember?"

"I did?"

"Of course you did. What were their names again?"

"James and Rachael."

"Yes, that's them. The ungrateful bastards."

"Oh, I must have told you. Funny, I don't remember."

"It's been a long trip, and you're a little tired."

"Yeah. I must be tired." Grandpa didn't say another word the rest of the trip, and neither did Jamie or Eddie.

The brigade of SUVs slowed down at the Brethren's gates long enough for the gates to open, and they drove through before stopping. The gate closed and Gideon commanded through the speakers, "All right, everyone, this is the end of the road."

Everyone got out and they were ushered to a tall and good-looking gentleman dressed in white linen from head to toe. "Faithfuls, may God's grace be upon you. My name is Obadiah, and on behalf of our great leader, Mordecai, I welcome you to the Brethren and the beginning of your new lives." His voice was smooth and lilting. He sounded like a public radio announcer.

Women dressed in drab woolen clothes appeared from nowhere. Obviously, their job was to take a more personal interest in the passengers. Or rather, take the passenger's personal interests. They collected the bags and luggage.

"At the Brethren, there are no personal belongings. What belongs to me belongs to everyone," a good-looking woman in a dark skirt told them. "It is easier for a camel to go through a needle's eye than a rich man to enter into the kingdom of heaven."

"My cell phone!" someone cried.

"Do not worry," the woman said. "You will learn to praise God in silent wonder and admiration."

Then they took Eddie's duffel bag, along with the medicine for his legs. Jamie was about to complain, but Eddie silenced him with a quick movement of his hand. It was none too soon, because in the distance another man yelled, "That's my medicine! I need my medicine. I have a heart condition!"

"Why such protestations?" Obadiah asked, walking up to the objecting man. Obadiah's voice was still calm and lilting, but loud enough for the entire group to hear.

"I need my medicine," the man complained. "Don't you understand? I'm ill."

"You have no need of medicine here, for Mordecai will restore your health. He has the ability to heal us of our wounds."

"Praise be to Mordecai," the good-looking woman said. She turned to the crowd and raised her arms, prompting them to join in.

Everyone raised their arms in return, like they were doing the wave at a football stadium. "Praise be to Mordecai."

Then Obadiah spoke again. "It is now time to partake in our most sacred sacrament. Baptism. As we follow the biblical precepts of the rite, each baptismal candidate enters his relationship with the Brethren with no outward vestiges of the greedy, self-indulgent world."

The women Faithfuls were separated from the men. Once apart, they whisked the women away. Obadiah looked over the men's group and proclaimed, "The rite of Baptism is the initiation into a world of righteousness."

Something came over the Faithfuls. In unison, they started

reciting, "Mordecai is great. Mordecai is good. Mordecai will redeem me of my sins." They also started pushing and shoving and tearing at each other's clothes until all that was left was their underwear.

"I want to be closer to salvation," a middle-aged man cried, falling to his knees.

Another man dug his fingernails into his cheeks, and blood started flowing onto his fingers. He cried, "Vanity is sinful."

"Wealth must be shunned," cried another. He pulled off his underpants and stood in the madding crowd, naked.

Then everyone started pleading, "Baptize me in the spirit of the Brethren."

Jamie was shocked. He looked over at Eddie, who shook his head. The converted Faithfuls, quiet and reserved in the SUVs, were raucous and without shame. Everyone, except for the shy teenager. He stood by himself, shaking.

Out of instinct, Jamie signaled the kid to join him. He obliged and started inching his way. But once they were together, several older Faithfuls grabbed them, tore off their outer clothes, and hustled them to the river.

Obadiah stood in the middle of the icy water, disregarding the state of his white linen uniform. One by one, he grabbed near-naked Faithfuls by the shoulders and dunked their heads into the creek. He didn't bother covering their noses and mouths with his hand or even a towel.

"I baptize you into the fold of the Brethren," he proclaimed. As he dunked, the Faithfuls would kick and flail.

When Obadiah pulled the Faithfuls out of the water, they each said "Alleluia." Then he pushed that Faithful out of the way and signaled for another one.

It was finally time for the teenager to be baptized. An old man grabbed him by the wrists and started pulling him into the river. The kid shook like a child lost in a supermarket. Jamie had enough of this barbarism. At the top of his lungs he cried, "Stop!"

Obadiah held out his arms, and Jamie started walking into the water. "We entered the gates of the Brethren together. And that's how we'll be baptized."

Eddie followed him in. Jamie could tell the cold water was doing a number on his leg, but he continued walking until he reached Jamie and the kid. Jamie put his arms around Eddie and the kid, and they stood there, resolute.

Obadiah gave Jamie a look that could kill, but didn't say anything. He took them into his large embrace and proceeded to submerse them into the river.

After a good twenty seconds of near drowning, Obadiah raised them to the surface. Jamie saw Eddie try to stand up in the water. He couldn't, and started falling back into the current. Luckily, Jamie caught him.

Eddie said, "Thank you, swee..." He stopped mid-word, but a look of horror flashed on his face. Jamie remained silent and hoped no one heard. Then he saw Obadiah glaring at them. He must have heard, yet didn't say anything. He looked toward the sky and yelled, "Alleluia."

In return, Jamie quietly repeated "Alleluia" and started walking back with Eddie and the teen.

The shy teenager didn't seem so apprehensive anymore.

CHAPTER TWELVE

"Alleluia," Zacchaeus cried as he ran from his secret clearing in the woods.

He liked hiding at the clearing, which overlooked the river. He especially liked it when the new Faithfuls were being baptized. Of course, if he got caught he would tell the Brethren he enjoyed watching the Faithfuls reach out to God, but that wasn't true. Deep in his heart, he realized that seeing men in their underwear—good-looking men, that is—excited him.

Today he had even more reason to be excited. He had pride, though he could never express it. Having lust was sinful enough. He had no idea what punishment would come from committing the sins of lust and pride at the same time. Today, however, they were wrapped up into one giant feeling of elation. Raamiah was wrong. He didn't chase Eddie and Jamie away. They had arrived at the Brethren.

And they would become the true saviors.

He quickly ran down the trail, pushing aside branches that weren't quite budding. He suddenly thought of a more earthly concern. It was dark. He had finished the laundry, but he still had the Disciples' mending to do. There'd be hell to pay if he got behind in his chores and caused the Disciples to be late for their exercises.

Then another kind of hell blocked his path. Raamiah.

"Well, well, well," Raamiah said, circling him. "Looks like your boyfriends made it, after all."

Zacchaeus started shaking again. He hated the feeling inside him. "I don't know what you're talking about, Disciple Raamiah."

"Don't you?"

"No."

"Well, let me put it in a way even a simpleton like you could understand." Raamiah smiled and grabbed Zacchaeus's crotch. He squeezed so hard it hurt. "I did you a favor. A big favor. And I'm not about to let that favor get me into trouble. Do you understand?"

"I think I do."

Raamiah squeezed again. The pain was excruciating. "Well, just so you do. You wouldn't want a misunderstanding to cause misfortune for your boyfriends, would you?"

"No."

"Good. So let me tell you how this is all going down. Okay?"

Zacchaeus could only nod.

"I'm gonna watch your boyfriends close. Real close. One misstep, one word out of turn, and they're gonna have an unfortunate accident. You get my drift?"

"Yes, sir."

"Good." Raamiah released him and wiggled his finger back and forth in front of Zacchaeus's face. "Then you'd better be on your way."

Zacchaeus couldn't reveal himself to Eddie or Jaime. Not now. Not after his run-in with Raamiah. He started worrying if they'd be able to figure out why they were sent for, or what their mission was supposed to be. He started running to the Disciples' quarters as fast as he could.

"Just one more thing," Raamiah called out. Zacchaeus stopped, but was too afraid to turn around. Raamiah continued shouting, "I'm afraid some kind of animal got into the Disciples' laundry when you were up in the woods jerking off. Did a number on all the clothes. Looks like you're gonna have a long night 'cause you're gonna have to do the laundry all over again."

Raamiah laughed and Zacchaeus ran even faster.

CHAPTER THIRTEEN

Jamie and Eddie, still just wearing their wet underwear, returned to the camp's entryway with everyone else. Their clothes had been taken away, and in their place were piles of linen garments. Gray pullover shirts and drawstring pants. Grubbies. Clean and neatly folded, but uniforms for manual labor all the same. They put on their work clothes with everyone else. And like everyone else, they looked Amish.

Another man took over. He carried a huge metal clipboard with a compartment on the bottom—the kind doctors used before they got iPads. "My name is Brother Saul, and I'll be making the dormitory assignments. Usually we do this after our blessed leader, Mordecai, gives everyone a tour of the Brethren. But given today's lateness, the tour will be postponed until tomorrow morning."

Saul gave Gideon a scornful look, and Gideon stared at the ground. "Women should go with Sister Elizabeth, while the men stay here."

The women were hustled out once again. Brother Saul told the men, "Follow me, and in the footsteps of all the Brethren before you."

They went into a huge building across the compound. "These are your dormitories," he explained. Using the plural was a misnomer, however. It was only one building separated into dozens of sections by curtains hung on wires. Each wing had a restroom, a line of four toilets. No dividers between them, and no privacy. The showers were just as bad, and had only cold water.

In the sleeping area were rows of numbered bunk beds, three high. One woolen blanket per bunk. No sheets or pillows, though.

Jamie looked at Eddie. "Not exactly five-star, is it?" He looked over at the shy kid, who was almost in tears.

Saul continued his instructions. "I'm going to hand out cards with numbers on them. These numbers correspond with your bunk assignments."

They lined up with the other men. Jamie got 115, Eddie 116. They'd be together. Jamie looked over at the kid, who held up his number, 69. It took all of Jamie's resolve to keep from laughing.

There was a huge commotion at the entryway, and everyone watched Obadiah storm up to Saul and Gideon. He whispered something to them, and the three moved away from the Faithfuls. Jamie watched as Saul opened up his clipboard and looked through his notes.

Saul returned to Jamie and Eddie and took the numbers out of their hands. "Excuse me," he said. "But there seems to have been a clerical error. We're missing some names on our roster."

Saul pointed to the shy boy. "What's your name, young man?"

"Peter Sokolov," he said.

"Ah, yes. I remember you." He looked at his notes and gave him back his number. Then he turned back to Jamie and Eddie. "Then who are you two?"

"Us?" Jamie asked.

"Nobody else here, is there?"

"Well, my name is Jamie Bradford." He stuck out his hand for a shake, but Saul didn't comply.

"And I'm Eddie Delgado."

Saul looked at them, then at his paperwork. He even made a show of opening up his clipboard to check additional papers.

"Tsk," he said loudly and made a bigger show of not finding what he was supposed to be looking for. "It appears we don't have either of your names on our lists. How could that be?"

Jamie shrugged his shoulders. "Gee. I don't know."

Saul gave him an evil-looking sneer. "It would have to be a pretty big clerical error if we left off two names, wouldn't it?"

Jamie said, "Well, it has to be an error. After all, Brother Gideon seems like a great commander, and I doubt he'd make a mistake like that out of negligence." Jamie looked over at Gideon and smiled.

"I wasn't accusing Brother Gideon of anything," Saul said. "I'm accusing you."

"Me?"

"Yes, you."

"But didn't one of your men check us in at the gates?"

Saul remained stone-faced.

"And weren't we baptized by one of your men?"

Saul glared at Obadiah and mumbled, "Yes, you were."

Jamie continued diplomatically. "So obviously, there must have been a simple misunderstanding somewhere in the line of command. Three highly organized soldiers of the Brethren don't make mistakes like that. After all, Eddie and I didn't appear out of nowhere."

"We don't make mistakes," Saul said stoically.

"Come on." Jamie lightly tapped Saul's paperwork. "Just put our names down on your list and give us back our bunk numbers."

"No," Saul said.

Gideon finally yelled, "Just give them their bunk numbers, Saul. That way Mordecai won't find out."

Saul frowned, but he wrote their names onto his list and handed the boys new numbers. He signaled his cohorts and the three men huffed off.

Jamie now had bunk number 412. Eddie had number 326. Not only were their beds far apart, they were in different wings.

But at least Jamie and Eddie weren't being thrown completely out of the Brethren.

They moved toward their assigned resting areas, and Peter asked, "See you guys tomorrow?"

"Where would we go?" Jamie said.

Peter smiled and left. When he was out of sight, Eddie whispered in Jamie's ear. "It may not be wise to consider him an ally."

"What?"

"That Peter kid. He was joining the Brethren, after all. His loyalties are probably more with them then they are to us."

"You're being paranoid. Peter's gay. He just doesn't admit it yet."

"Maybe. Maybe not. That's all I'm saying."

They walked in silence, stopping as Eddie turned in to the third wing.

Jamie reached out to give Eddie's cheek a light caress, then thought better of it. "Sorry," he said.

"No, you're right. Maybe I am paranoid."

"No, I said sorry about almost touching you. I have to be more careful because nothing's going right with this mission."

"How do you mean?"

"Well, you're probably right about Peter. We don't know him. And we won't be able to contact Ellen, either."

Eddie nodded. It looked like he was worried, too. Jamie looked around to be sure they were alone and then gave Eddie a quick kiss on the forehead. Eddie's face brightened, and he left for his wing.

Jamie finally felt good. Important. He and Eddie were on another mission. Ellen, too. Not exactly as dangerous or exotic as he imagined, but a mission all the same.

Jamie walked to the fourth wing and looked back. He saw Saul watching him from afar. Taking notes. Jamie didn't know if he'd seen the kiss, but he worried and made his own mental note. *Watch out for Brother Saul, the Clipboard Man.*

CHAPTER FOURTEEN

Christian couldn't meet with Ellen that night. He had to contact potential security firms, so they made plans for the next day. She called Marianne and asked about her father's schedule, hoping to have a late dinner with him. He was already booked, but Marianne promised to let her know if he became available.

Determined to put her time to good use, she checked into her condominium, one of several Rhodes Petroleum leased for new executive employees. Only a few blocks from the Rhodes building, it was convenient and plush. But most important, the protestors weren't picketing there.

The first thing she did was call Jamie. The call went to voicemail. But it was only the first day, and she knew they could take care of themselves.

Besides, what harm can a delusional preacher do? Right now, they're probably singing "Kumbayah" by a campfire. She looked at Jamie and Eddie's picture in her contact list and hoped she wasn't fooling herself. *They were supposed to call me by now. It's not like my boys to forget about something that important.*

She shuddered at the words she used. *My boys.* They weren't *her boys*. They were close friends. And they would never be anything more than that. *They're the fabulous gay couple, and I'm their good friend. Their fag hag.*

She hated that phrase, but made herself say it out loud. "Fag hag."

A tear rolled down her cheek, which she wiped away. She wasn't going to cry over her situation. She became determined to remedy it. And to do that, she needed to be rational and face the problem head-on.

She'd never find a meaningful romantic relationship if all the men she hung around with were gay.

Thoughts about Christian ran through her mind and made her nervous. He was handsome and she was attracted to him. But would the interest be reciprocal? She hoped to find out after she was finished with her investigation.

She set up her office, taking her laptop and cell phone out of her backpack. The suite already came equipped with necessities. Fax, printer, copier, all connected with a dedicated T1 line. Evidently, every Rhodes suite had its own high-speed communication access to Rhodes Petroleum. *A little overkill*, Ellen thought as she logged on to their private network.

She quickly found the PI's initial investigation of the Brethren. The boring stuff: land deeds, certificates of incorporation, their application for IRS tax exemption, and the appeals they filed when it was denied. One interesting fact did pop up. The IRS determined that the Brethren served the private interests of one individual, Mordecai (no last name on record). He and a couple of other "ministers" appeared to be the only paid employees. She wondered if they had other, under-the-table remuneration.

She searched the web for clues but only came across the same stuff that Jamie found. She did find some additional background, however, by clicking a resource link on the Brethren's wiki page. She burrowed down into that site and discovered a link to a document that wasn't listed on any of the search engines. It didn't have a title or even say who the author was. She clicked the hyperlink, and her browser warned that downloading the file might harm her computer.

What do I have to lose, except maybe my laptop? Holding

her breath, she pressed *continue*. The screen flashed white. A new box appeared and the computer launched another document containing a scholarly overview of the Brethren. It said the cult took the basic concepts of Christianity, added some hocus-pocus dogma into the mix, and turned the cult's leader, Mordecai, into God's divine prophet.

A potential convert's first few encounters with the Brethren made the organization look like heaven. If they joined, they would become Mordecai's assistants and be instrumental in saving the world from evil. And of course, they would be rewarded in heaven for their work.

But once inside the Brethren's compound, life became harsh. Admission into heaven was based on how hard they toiled for Mordecai. To maintain control, the leaders used coercion and violence.

Ellen scrolled down the page and read about the biblical Mordecai. He was a prophet in the Old Testament who saved his tribe from being massacred.

The Brethren's Mordecai was very different. His real name was Thomas Jackson from Green County, Kentucky. He used to travel around that state, setting up a tent and preaching hellfire and damnation. He lived off the proceeds of his collection plate. Then he disappeared for a while and reemerged as Mordecai. His popularity and revenue soared.

Below that section was a paragraph in red text, and a much larger font. When Ellen read the section, her chest constricted so tightly she couldn't breathe.

Beware! Mordecai believes he is the First Horseman of the Apocalypse. "I looked, and there before me was a white horse! Its rider held a bow, and he was given a crown, and he rode out as a conqueror bent on conquest." Mordecai believes he is Christ, spreading the Gospel. But he isn't. He is the Antichrist.

She read it several times and decided whoever had written that part was as delusional as Mordecai. Why would he adopt the name of a hero if he wanted to destroy the world? It didn't make sense, even for a crazy street preacher.

She attempted to save the text onto her computer, but the application didn't have a menu bar, so she pressed the *print screen* button on her keyboard. The screen flashed white and the document disappeared. Shocked, she went to her web browser and pressed the link to download it again. An error message appeared. *The document you requested cannot be found.* She looked at the browser. It didn't list a URL, only an IP address. She highlighted the numbers to copy them, but the screen flashed again. Her browser shut down, corrupted.

Freaked, she scanned her computer for viruses, but it came up clean.

First thing tomorrow, I'm bringing this laptop in to be looked at. She powered down and went to bed, hoping Jamie would call.

CHAPTER FIFTEEN

Holy Tuesday

Before the sun rose, the Brethren's speakers bellowed loud enough to raise Lazarus from the dead—or at least enough to get the Faithfuls up from their sleep.

Jamie didn't have to wake up. He couldn't fall asleep because he was worried about not being able to call Ellen. And on top of that, there must be a shooting range close to the Brethren, because gunfire rang out all night long.

Despite being fully awake, he still had trouble getting out of his bunk. His was on the top, and there wasn't a ladder. The mattress wasn't filled with cotton or foam, either. It was stuffed with horse hair. When he got down, he shook the kinks out of his back and ran to Eddie's assigned wing. Luckily, Eddie got a bottom bunk, but his mattress didn't look any better.

Jamie asked, "How'd you sleep?"

"Horribly," Eddie replied. He pulled up his linen shirt and exposed tiny red bumps all over his stomach. "I think my mattress has fleas."

"Oh, my poor sweetie."

Eddie nodded with resignation. Then he started to scratch his bites, but Jamie brushed his hand away. "Don't touch them. That'll only make them fester."

They didn't have time to worry about infestations, though. Peter Sokolov found them before they had a chance. He yelled, "How you guys doing?" His voice was as nasal as it had been the night before. Peter ran to them, his arms in the air.

Jamie gave Eddie an *I-told-you-so* kind of look, but Eddie quickly shook his head and pulled down his shirt. "We're doing okay," Eddie told Peter casually.

"Speak for yourself," Jamie piped in, ready to recite a diatribe. "Personally, I…"

Eddie coughed. Jamie remembered last night's conversation and took the hint. "Well, I'm starving."

One of the old-time Faithfuls must have overheard them talking. "How can you fellas think about food? From what I heard, you haven't had your tour or even been assigned your mission in life." He got up from his bunk and rolled up his mattress, sticking it at the foot of his bed.

"Thanks," Jamie said. "But before I do anything, I have to go to the bathroom."

Jamie went to the non-private toilets. All he could think about was the degradation of having to do his business in front of everyone, not to mention the smell. But he realized that was probably the Brethren's intent—to dehumanize their Faithfuls.

When he was done, he joined Eddie and the rest of the men. They rallied with the women in the main square and were ordered to stand at attention while they waited for Mordecai. They waited with the patience of saints for what seemed like hours, and they weren't even allowed to sit during that time.

"What if the rapture were to happen and God found you lollygagging on your butts?" Saul said. "God would think you weren't expecting him, and he'd pass you by. Would you treat Mordecai with any less respect than you treat God?"

The Faithfuls shook their heads.

"I didn't think so."

They remained standing. Yet as the minutes went by,

perspiration started rolling down Eddie's forehead. He shifted his weight from one leg to another, but he didn't complain about the pain.

Jamie wished Eddie still had the medicine for his leg, but the Brethren had tossed it out last night. Then he got an ingenious idea. He and Eddie still stood at attention, but they stood with their backs to each other. They used each other for support and they weren't sitting or lying on the ground. Soon enough, all the Faithfuls caught on to their trick and were doing the same thing.

The guards didn't say anything. Jamie figured it was probably because none of the rules were technically being broken.

After another half hour of leaning, celestial music finally played from the speakers. Everyone raised their hands into the air and reworked yesterday's wave bit. "Praise be to Mordecai," they recited in unison. "Mordecai is Great. Mordecai is good. Mordecai will redeem me of my sins." They repeated it over and over in a deafening fortissimo.

From a distance, a man with fair skin and dark, curly hair walked into the middle of the square. He held up his hand. "Please, I am undeserving of such acclamation. For I am merely a messenger."

Obviously, this was Mordecai. He was barefoot and his clothes were white, not gray. He wore a red sash tied around his waist. It looked like silk.

When the crowd settled down, Mordecai selected a woman from the crowd. He pulled a flower from his pocket and placed it in her hair. She blushed, and Mordecai gently brought her face to his. "Like Jesus before me, no one can experience Heaven but through me."

This guy is obsessed with himself, Jamie thought.

Mordecai stopped fondling the woman and walked into the middle of the crowd. Some of the Faithfuls fell to their knees. They reached out and touched his feet like they would a venerated saint.

Jamie wanted to laugh, but the whole thing sickened him.

Mordecai addressed the crowd. "At the Brethren, we extol the virtues of simple life. Away from worldly sins and temptations."

There was an uncomfortable pause, which Saul filled. "Tell us, O esteemed religious leader, why is the Brethren so concerned with shunning worldly comforts?"

"Because the riches we seek wait for us in heaven."

"Isn't that hard to accomplish?"

"Extremely difficult, even for me." Mordecai chuckled and the Faithfuls laughed, too.

"Personally, I would love to wallow in the luxuries of this world. Electricity. Television with cable. A cell phone. But you know what God tells me every day? 'Mordecai,' he says, 'the Brethren is the only pathway to achieve heaven's treasures.' And he's right, you know. Because he's God."

Mordecai gave them all a wide grin, and the crowd applauded again. A woman interrupted the ovation. "Oh, great Mordecai, help me. I suffer from a terrible cancer."

Mordecai got even more theatrical. He knelt down and took her hand. "This disease is a sin that is destroying your body and your soul. Where is this scourge located, my child?"

"The doctors say I have ovarian cancer. But it is too advanced and they can't cure me."

"Your doctors are right. They can't heal you, my child. But I can." Mordecai embraced the woman. "Doctors believe only in science. They don't believe in the miracles of the Brethren."

He rubbed her abdomen with his hands. "But your faith in the Brethren and God will set you free from this horrible disease."

He rubbed harder and harder. Then he looked up into the heavens. "I renounce the devil within this woman's body. And I command that evil to leave her sinful vessel at once."

Mordecai started crying as if he was in pain, and the woman cried in return. Mordecai convulsed, and so did she. Finally, the woman fell to the ground and Mordecai followed, landing on top of her.

"You're cured," he pronounced.

"I'm cured," she yelled between her cries. "Praise Mordecai, I'm cured."

"Yes. By renouncing your sins and by embracing the Brethren's righteous ways, you have defeated evil." Mordecai rose and gazed at the crowd. They watched back in wonder. It seemed like Mordecai's blue eyes pierced the soul of everyone.

He walked over to Eddie. "Are you a gimp, my child?"

Eddie said nothing.

"It's a simple question, boy. Can't you answer a simple question?"

"Yes, sir." Eddie paused a moment. "You're correct. I have a limp."

"How did you incur God's wrath?"

"I didn't do anything, sir. It was an accident."

"You did nothing to deserve your malady?" Mordecai smirked and the crowd laughed. "With God, there are no accidents, boy. Only punishments, so you had to do something."

"I don't understand, sir."

The crowd's laughter increased. "You don't understand God's curse? What are you, an imbecile?" The laughter turned loud and unruly. "Disease. Injury. Death. These are a part of your life because you refuse to accept the way of the Brethren."

"Perhaps you're right, sir."

"Perhaps? Perhaps I'm right?"

"I'm sorry. You're right, sir. I refused to accept the way of the Brethren."

Mordecai turned to the crowd and grinned. Then he embraced Eddie. "That's okay, my child. You just took the first step. You've admitted your sinful ways and have started to travel down the righteous path, the way of the Brethren."

Jamie remained silent during Eddie's ordeal, but he hated himself for not standing up to Mordecai. He'd seen his type before. He was a bully, and Jamie had his fill of them growing up in Wisconsin.

One of the new Faithfuls asked, "O great Mordecai, what is the Brethren's way?"

Mordecai walked over to him. "There isn't a simple answer to your question, my child. But discovering the answer is the only way we can reap God's treasures and gain his wisdom and knowledge."

This guy's talking in circles, Jamie thought.

"Then how do I find the answer?" the Faithful asked.

Mordecai spread his arms out wide. "You have to reject wealth and the pleasures of the body. You must give yourself to the Brethren and live apart from the sinful world."

That was it for Jamie. "Excuse me, Mr. Mordecai, but the principles you're extolling don't make sense to me."

Mordecai's peaceful countenance changed. "What things don't make sense, my…" He looked at Jamie, and with a staccato in his voice, repeated, "What are the things that don't make sense?"

"The SUVs. The loudspeakers. They're modern conveniences. And your guards patrolling the area with their big guns. This doesn't match your philosophy of rejecting the pleasures of the world. Does it?"

"How little you know, my little man," Mordecai bellowed. "These conveniences—the inconsistencies that you point out— are necessary to maintain the Brethren's presence on earth. We don't use them to better ourselves or make our lives easier. We use them to survive."

"To survive?" Jamie wondered.

"The world despises my special relationship with God. They want me and the Brethren eliminated."

Jamie couldn't make sense of what he was hearing. "Eliminated?"

"Of course. Exterminated. Annihilated. Stamped off the face of the earth. Don't I have a right to protect my flock? To keep evil from entering my doorway?"

Jamie nodded and Mordecai continued forcefully. "Oh, rest assured, God has given me the power to smite any who oppose me." He raised his hands above Jamie, then stopped and looked at the Faithfuls around him and lowered his hands. "But I wouldn't do that, because it's against our principles."

Mordecai's demeanor changed. No longer energetic, he seemed emotionally spent. "That's enough for now. I'm sure all your heads are spinning. We'll assemble again after taking nourishment."

Mordecai turned around and left the crowd, his red sash trailing behind him. Saul followed.

Eddie looked over at Jamie and whispered, "We're going to eat before our duties are assigned? They're breaking their own rules again."

"Evidently, Mordecai is allowed to do that," Jamie said.

CHAPTER SIXTEEN

Mordecai charged away from the square, his head throbbing with pain. But he couldn't let the Faithfuls see his distress. God's Holy emissary doesn't suffer. Besides, he knew his headache wasn't a result of God's vengeance. His condition was caused by a devil's ploy, implemented by a greedy weasel who refused to accept his divinity. He'd encountered this before. The first time was at the seminary when his teachers called him emotionally disturbed. And now he was experiencing it again with that snake, Saul.

Saul must have known this group of Faithfuls was rancorous, yet he did nothing to prepare him. Saul would pay for his sins. But his judgment day would have to wait because he was needed. So for now, Mordecai would play along with Saul's little game.

Mordecai reached his office, hidden away from the rest of the Brethren, and paused to remember the entryway's code, then punched it in. The steel-reinforced door gave way. Saul followed behind, apologetically closed the door, and punched in another code to bolt the entrance.

Mordecai ripped off his sash and threw it on his desk. "Well, this is going hellish, and it's your fault. You shouldn't have brought in so many new Faithfuls this close to the mission."

"I'm sorry, but it's the mission that's depleting our cash

reserves. This group brought in nearly seven hundred thousand dollars."

Mordecai's demeanor perked. *If this amount is accurate,* he thought, *perhaps Saul isn't so evil after all.* "God has certainly provided in our time of need. How many new Faithfuls are there, anyway?"

"Seventy-five."

The number almost made Mordecai happy. "Where did Gideon put them all?"

"I have no idea. But thank goodness he found the room—although I'm sure goodness had nothing to do with it." Saul laughed. Mordecai didn't, already fantasizing about how he'd use the increased manpower and cash.

Daydreaming could be dangerous, though. If he lost his aura of superiority, he'd lose his advantage over the Faithfuls. "Yes, we're making improvements in the conversion area. But there are other matters to be concerned with." He walked to the wall safe and punched in the combination. Inside, he searched for his computer's security hardware, but couldn't find it. Frantic, he began throwing papers and documents around the safe while he searched. Positive Saul had hidden his equipment, he slammed his fist against the safe's door.

Saul calmly opened the desk drawer and pulled out a small USB-like accessory. "Is this what you're looking for? I noticed you didn't lock it up last night." Mordecai sneered at Saul and grabbed the hardware from his spindly little fingers. He inserted the piece into his CPU, the system booted, and the screen turned blue. He typed in his password and logged on.

As his first task, he searched through screens and screens of data logs. When he couldn't find the documents he wanted, he felt the pressure increasing exponentially inside his head.

"Any communication from him?" Saul asked.

"No. You'd think after the message he sent last night, an update isn't too much to ask from the guy. Especially considering what I'm paying him."

"Well, you're the one who doesn't trust e-mails, even with encryption. You had to go with a fancy program, with special hardware on the computers and everything."

"Even encrypted e-mails sent over the public Internet can be intercepted, Saul. Remember the surveillance worm we discovered last year? We got infected by e-mail, remember?" Saul gave him a slight nod. "This is better protection. It's a private pipeline going through several proxy servers daisy-chained together. It's completely anonymous. If only that infidel would use it." Mordecai threw his mouse at the monitor and sat back in his chair, deflated.

Saul walked over to him, acting almost like a friend rather than an employee. "Look, why don't you just call the guy with a prepaid phone?"

Mordecai hated unnecessary contact with humans. "We can't risk it. There isn't enough chatter in this area to hide our calls, and the Feds would easily figure out who we were."

"Well then, good things come to those who wait. Didn't Jesus say that?"

Mordecai scowled. "No, he didn't. So just shut up and pour me a drink."

"Red or white?"

"Surprise me."

Saul went to the liquor cabinet and returned with a filled crystal goblet. Mordecai smiled and said, "You first."

Saul took a gulp of wine and handed the glass back to him.

Mordecai relished his sip. "Chardonnay. Good choice." He always enjoyed wine. Jesus's drink of choice. Feeling generous, he nodded at a chair, granting Saul permission to sit.

Saul accepted the offer. "I don't know why you're so concerned with our conversion rate, anyway. After the mission, our numbers will skyrocket. Right?"

"God expects us to be concerned with each lost soul."

"Of course." Saul lowered his head, and Mordecai scowled at his humility. Saul concerned himself with numbers, not people—which was why he hired him. It takes all kinds to save souls, and sometimes the righteous had to partner with evil, if it accomplished God's work.

Mordecai took a deep breath, closed the transfer program on his computer, and opened iTunes. "So, cheer me up, Saul. Update me on the backgrounds of the new Faithfuls."

Saul grabbed his clipboard, and looked over the inventory of souls. "Well, pretty much normal stuff. A retired guy disappointed with his grandchildren. A few individuals searching for meaning in their lives. But we have one particularly bright spot on our list. His name's Peter Sokolov." Mordecai's face scrunched up, and Saul explained. "He's Eastern European. His father's on the board of a foreign banking commission, and reputedly, he's pretty corrupt."

"So I'm supposed to gush because of that?"

Saul gave Mordecai a conspiratorial smirk. "A Faithful whose family is strategically involved with world economics? Yeah, it could be worth a little gushing. I'd suggest assigning the kid to my division. Supposedly, he's good with computers."

"What makes you think you rank higher than the Disciples?"

"Follow the money and you'll know why."

"Well, my Disciples are infiltrating the enemy."

"But who brings in the cash to pay them?"

"I know." Mordecai took a sip of wine. "Your work is more than adequate, Saul. But sometimes it needs improvement."

"Improvement?"

"Yeah. Like the two fags. Tell me about them."

Saul looked flustered. "I'm sorry, the two who?"

"Don't play coy with me. The girly white boy and his feeble Latino friend. The two queers. What's their story?"

Saul looked through his notes and shrugged. "There really isn't much to tell. Our reconnaissance must have let us down on those two."

"Well then, you have some homework to do. Don't you?"

Mordecai picked up his sash and caressed it. Feeling the silky fabric calmed him. "Queers certainly have big mouths on them, don't they, Saul?"

"Yeah. And the prissy one has the biggest mouth I've ever seen."

Mordecai grinned as an idea percolated in his mind. "Does the girly boy have any friends here, besides the gimp?"

"Possibly that Peter kid," Saul said. "But he's so timid, I doubt anybody cares about him either. Why?"

Mordecai quickly wrapped the sash around Saul's neck and pulled it tight. "Because homos are against God's law and they deserve to die."

"Okay. I understand," Saul said, grasping his neck. "So you want me to have them killed?"

"No. Not yet." Mordecai removed the sash and began smoothing out the wrinkles. "He and his friend could be useful to us."

"How can two queers be useful to us?"

"If I had my way, I wouldn't rely on faggots. But we've got to use the tools God gives us. Tools like hate." Mordecai's grin started to grow. "People have an immediate dislike for others who are different. All we have to do is cultivate that dislike into something more powerful."

Saul grinned, too. "Ah, I understand."

"Good. And when everyone's hate is at its peak, I'll squash the faggots like little bugs and everyone will love me even more."

CHAPTER SEVENTEEN

After the meal, a gloppy gruel, the Faithfuls rallied for Mordecai's second installment. Jamie and Eddie trudged to the square and Peter pestered them the entire way. "Boy, that food really sucked, didn't it."

Jamie didn't know what to do. His first instinct was to answer Peter. He was lonely, and reaching out for friendship. But if Eddie's suspicions were right, it could be dangerous to get into a conversation with him. Jamie mumbled, "I dunno."

"Didn't you taste it?"

"Tasted like oatmeal to me."

"Well our cook at home always makes kasha. That's *her* oatmeal. And hers tastes way better than the stuff they made."

"A cook, huh?" Jamie made a mental note. The kid came from a wealthy family.

"But I'm not like them," Peter said quickly.

Jamie continued walking. Another note: *He's embarrassed about his family's wealth.* Jamie stopped and gave Peter a comforting pat on the shoulder. "That's okay. One of my best friends is wealthy, too."

"Really?"

"Yeah. And she's not bad at all."

Peter's eyes brightened, and then he looked crestfallen. "Then what's the matter with me?"

"Nothing's wrong with you," Jamie said. "You're a cool guy, except you ask too many questions."

"You think I'm cool?"

Jamie nodded and Peter gave him a smile that reached from one side of his face to the other. "Then I'll work at controlling my inquisitive nature."

"Thanks." Jamie looked over at Eddie. *See? Peter's not a spy. He's a closet case.*

Eddie gave him back a worried look.

Luckily, when they reached the square they didn't have to wait long for Mordecai. He entered with his usual pomp and circumstance, handing out flowers. Standing in the middle of the crowd, he raised his arms. "Labor is a fundamental part of the Brethren's precepts. Work paves our way into heaven."

Mordecai held out a piece of papyrus, and everyone watched him examine it carefully. "Peter Sokolov?" he called out. Peter walked up, and Mordecai grabbed hold of him. "Peter Sokolov, you are near and dear to my heart."

That statement made Jamie's ears pick up. Eddie's suspicions might be correct after all.

"Peter, you shall be assigned the important mission of assisting Saul."

He lowered his head. "Thank you, Mordecai." Disappointment was clear on his face as he returned to Jamie and Eddie.

Mordecai continued to assign duties to the rest of the Faithfuls. Some were to tend the fields and livestock, others to cook, and still others to clean. Then Mordecai called Jamie and Eddie up. "Your assignments are to muck out the horse stalls. Daily. Not only will it be backbreaking work, it'll be smelly, too."

Mordecai smiled, and Jamie and Eddie bowed their heads with the required subservience.

Then, all of a sudden, Peter asked, "Excuse me, O great

Mordecai. Will there ever be a change of positions, or are we going to be stuck in these professions forever?"

Mordecai answered, "No, Peter. Unless…"

"Unless what, sir?"

"Unless you achieve a higher level of consciousness."

"How do I reach a higher level?"

"I bestowed it on them." Mordecai pointed to living quarters on the other side of the square. It resembled a huge ski chalet. The porch even had Adirondack chairs. "So far, twelve of our most devoted followers have reached this level. They're my Disciples.

"But enough about that," Mordecai said. "The Brethren Names still have to be assigned. This is your new identity, which will follow you into heaven."

Eddie leaned over to Jamie and whispered, "Why rename everyone?"

"A psychological ploy," he answered. "So we stop thinking we had a life before joining the Brethren."

"Silence!" Mordecai yelled, and Jamie stood at attention. Mordecai cleared his throat and continued. "It is the name you will go by from this day forward. And without it, you won't be allowed through heaven's gates."

One by one, the Faithfuls went up to Mordecai. He took each person into his arms, embraced them, kissed them gently on the forehead, and gave them their new Brethren name.

Igal, the avenger. Thaddeus, the wise. Hannah, the graceful.

Then Peter walked up and Mordecai addressed him. "Ah, my special young man. I name you Caleb, from the tribe of Judah."

Jamie whispered to Eddie, "Who the hell is Caleb?"

His answer was disturbing. "He was a spy."

Eddie's suspicions were right. Peter, now Caleb, was a spy for the Brethren. But was he spying on them? That didn't seem possible. After all, no one had known they were coming. Not even the person who sent them the weird message.

Peter parted from Mordecai's embrace and walked back to Jamie and Eddie. "Caleb," he whispered. "What a cool name."

Then Mordecai commanded Jamie and Eddie to come forward. He took them into his embrace.

"You two have a long way to go before achieving supreme consciousness. So I give you the names Esrom and Roboam."

"Who are they?" Jamie asked.

"They're nobodies in the Bible. They're just two people in a long line of begets."

Eddie asked, "Did they do anything?"

"No. Nothing," was Mordecai's answer. "And unless you give your hearts and souls to me, you'll be just like them. And you'll die without mercy."

CHAPTER EIGHTEEN

Ellen sat on her bed, unable to shake from her mind the weird document she'd found online the previous night. The computer expert who looked at her laptop said nothing was wrong with it and that she'd probably downloaded an executable file that ran a programmed task. In this case, it deleted itself. And since it didn't leave a virus, she shouldn't worry about it.

Too much, at least.

But she wasn't going to take any chances. She backed up her computer to the cloud and wiped the hard drive clean. She planned to purchase a new computer at the first opportunity.

Christian had promised to stop by, so she grabbed her cell and sat by the window. To pass the time, she used her smartphone to surf the news sites, but her thoughts kept drifting back to Jamie and Eddie. They hadn't called yet, and she was worried.

Opening the speed dial, she touched Jamie's number. It rang and rang, and finally went to voicemail. She left the message, "Why don't you call me?" Exasperated, she swiped the screen closed and threw the phone onto her bed.

Then it rang with a Rufus Wainwright song. But she knew it wasn't the boys calling her. Their ringtone was Lady Gaga. Rufus meant that her computerized call-forwarding service didn't recognize the number. And since the caller didn't leave a name at the prompt, she figured it had to be a sales call. She let it go to voicemail and checked the time on her phone instead. Christian was late.

A couple of knocks came from the door, however. It was Christian, and he held out a small bouquet of flowers. *Why would he bring me flowers?* she asked herself. *We don't have that kind of relationship.* "Thank you."

"Sorry for being late," he said, taking a step inside. "I tried calling, but my calls kept going to voicemail."

Ellen quickly checked her cell and realized he must have been the private caller. "Now I feel dumb. My phone didn't recognize your number. I'm sorry."

"No, I'm sorry. It's been hectic this morning, I haven't gone into the office yet, so I called from my cell phone."

"I hope everything's okay," she said, getting a vase to put the flowers in.

"Actually, better. I found the perfect security firm for your father and spent the morning working out the final details with them. All that's left is to sign the contracts."

"Wow." She was amazed at Christian's efficiency. "And the legal department already gave the contracts a once-over?"

"We don't have the time for lawyers to get involved," he said, helping her with the flower arrangement. "Your father has a public appearance this weekend, and he told me we need to have security in place."

"Well, I bet it's going to cost Daddy a lot more than the old firm did."

"No, it's costing less." She looked up at Christian and saw pride on his face. "Rhodes Petroleum is a major player," he continued. "So new companies practically lined up for the chance to be taken advantage of." He laughed.

"You hired a new company?" That didn't sound like something her father would approve of, either.

"Well, the company's new, but their employees have been mercenaries for a long time."

"Mercenaries?" She made a nervous laugh, but her stomach

cringed at the thought of her father being protected by paid soldiers. *Then again*, she thought, *aren't most security people mercenaries in one-way or another?* They got paid to carry a gun, and probably very few worried about who their client was.

Christian looked at his watch. "We should get going."

"Where to?" she asked, slinging her backpack onto her shoulder.

"I thought we could go to Fenway Park. The Red Sox have an afternoon game, and Rhodes has a corporate box. I even hear Ben Affleck might throw out the opening pitch."

"Well, I really wanted to discuss some projects that Rhodes Petroleum has in Boston."

"We can do that at the game," Christian insisted. "We lease a corporate box at the ballpark with a conference table in it. And if you ask something I don't know, I can always look up the answer on my laptop." He held up his briefcase and gave it a pat.

Ellen smiled. "A handsome movie star and a Red Sox game? Who could pass up such a great combination?"

"Great. But please, call me Chris." He offered his arm and they left for the parking lot.

When they got outside, they found several doormen huddled around a shining BMW Z4 Roadster. Impressed, Ellen asked, "This is yours?"

He smiled.

❖

Ellen didn't learn much about Rhodes Petroleum at the game, but she had a blast with Chris. Boston won, and they left Fenway Park in a heated discussion.

"For my money," he said, "Cy Young was the Red Sox's best pitcher."

"How can you say that?" she countered. "Especially when they had Smoky Joe Wood and Pedro Martinez?"

Waiting for traffic to clear at an intersection, he said, "I'm impressed. A gorgeous woman who knows about baseball."

She gave him a demure smile. But when they got to Chris's car, she wanted to get back to work. "We didn't get much done in terms of Rhodes Petroleum, you know."

"Well, I actually have an appointment," he told her, tapping his watch. "But if you'd like, we can talk more tonight. Over dinner, perhaps?"

Ellen didn't want to postpone working, but she did like the idea of dinner with Chris. They encountered heavy traffic on the interstate, and Chris had to inch his way along slowly. Traffic came to a complete stop in front of a huge billboard. It had a picture of Jesus leaving his tomb, and written in a fancy font was *Discover the true meaning of Easter. Join us for the National Easter Sunrise Service in Boston. Televised Live!* On the bottom in smaller lettering was *The American Council of Conservative Christians.*

"Boy," Ellen said. "It looks like Easter is going to bring out the conservative faction."

"Yeah, and traffic will be a mess, 'cause the world will be filled with crazies."

She looked at Christian with surprise. *That's the phrase Daddy used.*

CHAPTER NINETEEN

A children's Bible song comforted Zacchaeus, so he sang it over and over. "Zacchaeus was a wee little man. A wee little man was he…"

The tune gave him a sense of place in the world, a sense of his responsibilities. He vowed not to worry about Eddie Delgado and Jamie Bradford. They would know what needed to be done and just had to wait until the time came.

Besides, he particularly liked today's duties, away from Raamiah and his dirty tricks. Sitting on the edge of a whirlpool bathtub so large it almost occupied the entire room, he knew what to do. He was the Disciples' manservant, and his only mission was to care for them. He set thick towels by the whirlpool's edge. He rolled up his sleeve and dipped his wrist in the water to test its temperature. He adjusted the tub's air streams so the bubbles wouldn't be too intrusive. Today, the bath had to be just right because it was for Sharar, the head Disciple.

Zacchaeus worried that his affection for Sharar was sinful, that he liked him too much. Sharar was strong, handsome, and caring. Sharar only did bad things when the Lord's work required it.

Footsteps sounded in the hall and he opened the door. It was Sharar, wearing a linen robe. Zacchaeus bowed and Sharar entered, dropping his robe on the floor as he walked to the bath.

Zacchaeus picked up the garment and closed the door. Keeping his eyes on the floor while Sharar stepped into the bathwater took all his resolve, but he still imagined the strong muscles of Sharar's back, the hair on his firm legs and the softer hair on his buttocks.

Sharar splashed in the water and said, "Ah. The temperature is perfect."

"Thank you, Disciple." He kept his head down while addressing Sharar. Not out of fear or trepidation, but out of respect. Many of the faithful feared Sharar, but not Zacchaeus. Sharar wasn't the enemy. He was a warrior for the Brethren.

Zacchaeus began to move back to the supply table, but Sharar stopped him. "I didn't excuse you, did I?"

He froze. "No, sir."

"I still have need of you, Zacchaeus. Come here."

He returned to Sharar's side with a cloth and soap in hand. Dipping the cloth into the warm water, he worked the soap into a lather and gently rubbed his Disciple's back.

"Harder," Sharar instructed. "Go deep into my muscles."

He rubbed with all his might, but still Sharar requested he use more force.

"Maybe if you were in the water with me," Sharar suggested.

Zacchaeus hesitated, not sure how to respond. He said softly, "But it wouldn't be right, Disciple."

"Then keep your clothes on, if you insist. But come next to me."

He held his breath and did as Sharar commanded. He walked into the water fully clothed. Embarrassed by the way his linen clothing clung to his body, he kept a respectable distance. He tried not to think of Sharar, inches away, naked. He tried to think only of his duty. He rubbed Sharar's back with even more force.

"You're still not going deep enough," Sharar said. "Perhaps if you came closer."

He hesitantly nudged next to Sharar's back. The intimacy

excited him, and his body's reaction embarrassed him. Sharar must have felt his hardness, his sin.

Yet Sharar said nothing.

Finally, his embarrassment was too much. He separated from Sharar and covered his loins with his hands. "I'm sorry," he said.

"There's nothing to feel sorry about," Sharar said calmly, as if he were chatting about the weather. "Your reaction was natural, given to you by God. You shouldn't be ashamed of what God gives you."

Zacchaeus wanted to believe him, but couldn't. Too many people had told him otherwise. "That's not what Mordecai preaches."

"And do you believe everything Mordecai says?"

"Of course I do."

"That's where you and I differ." Sharar laughed and leaned back on Zacchaeus's chest. "Sometimes a little sin can be a holy experience."

Zacchaeus became frightened. His hands started shaking. "I don't believe that."

"Well, rest your head on my shoulder and tell me how it feels."

Zacchaeus obeyed. He snuggled in closer and placed his cheek in the crook of Sharar's neck. He shut his eyes and breathed in the scent of Sharar's skin.

"So, how does it feel?" Sharar asked.

"It feels good."

"See? I wouldn't lie to you. You're my little soldier."

He was surprised at the comment. "I'm your soldier?"

"Didn't I tell you? I want you to attend the field exercises, starting tonight. You'll even go on our next mission." Sharar stood, grasped Zacchaeus's hands, and drew him to his feet. "And if everything goes well, you won't be a manservant any longer. You'll become a Disciple."

"A thirteenth Disciple? Is that even allowed?"

"Why wouldn't it be? I make the rules," Sharar said. "Now, get me my towel."

Zacchaeus scrambled out of the whirlpool and began drying his Disciple's back. It felt natural attending to Sharar, the way God intended. But deep down he feared the feeling wouldn't last long, and he trembled at what would happen at their next mission.

CHAPTER TWENTY

Ellen sat at the bar of the fashionable restaurant L'Epicurean, reviewing more documents from the private investigator. She was anxious to start her investigation with Christian. He'd promised to meet her when his meetings ended.

He certainly keeps busy, she thought while writing down notes on her tablet. *That's probably why Daddy likes him so much.* She wondered if her father would still like him if they were seeing each other on a personal level. She didn't know. She wasn't even sure she wanted to get involved with Christian anymore. He never seemed to be around when needed.

She looked around the fancy restaurant and another concern entered her mind. Even though this evening's meeting would be on her father's tab, Christian's lifestyle seemed more upscale than his salary should allow. *But I guess that's none of my business.*

Chris arrived, and she put aside her concerns. They shared some wine and cheese while their table was being prepared. "I'm disappointed," she said. "I was hoping we'd be well into the investigation by this time, but we haven't even begun."

"Well, I'll try my best to help," Christian said. "But you need to be specific about what you're investigating. You only say that you're 'searching for a connection' or something equally vague."

"I'm sorry." His comment didn't completely surprise her since she wasn't sure what she was looking for. Perhaps she needed to start at the very beginning, in very general terms. No need to show her hand, at least not until she knew him better. "I'm hoping to find out if Rhodes Petroleum has any connection to a religious cult based in New York. It's called the Brethren."

She looked into Chris's eyes and saw his pupils contract. Then he started coughing uncontrollably. She offered him a napkin and patted his back. Even the waiter came to their side, but he dismissed him with a wave of his hand.

He coughed a little more, and the emergency subsided. "Sorry," he said, blinking and shaking his head little. "A piece of cheese went down the wrong way."

She took another breath and started again. "I need to know if the Brethren might be involved with Daddy's company. Even the smallest connection might be a clue."

"The Brethren?" He shook his head and raised his eyebrows. "Can't say that I recall ever hearing anything about them. But Rhodes Petroleum is pretty big, and I'm new."

Ellen nodded, but she prodded him for more information. He finally said, "Since Rhodes Petroleum is a for-profit corporation, perhaps the connection you're looking for is financial? A business deal of some kind?"

"I wondered about that, but according to the company's accountants, the Brethren isn't a vendor or a customer of Rhodes Petroleum. And the private investigator reports that the Brethren isn't involved with oil, or even real estate. So what kind of relationship could they have?"

"Maybe it's not a business relationship. Perhaps the connection involves philanthropy."

It made sense. "Okay, what nonprofit organizations does the company support?"

"Well, your father covers his bases. He gives to liberal causes along with conservative ones."

"I don't understand," she said. "Doesn't Daddy have a mission statement that guides what kinds of donations he makes?"

"No. His only guideline is the potential for payback. But that's why many companies donate money. They want to make sure that no matter who is in office, or what philosophical faction may be popular at the time, their company's welfare will be safeguarded."

"You don't believe in sugarcoating things, do you, Chris?"

"Sorry, but in business every donation is self-serving in some way or another."

"I don't believe that." When the waiter approached, saying their table was ready, Ellen stood up and grabbed her backpack. "Daddy's gifts do good, too."

"Of course they do. Philanthropy betters the course of mankind. But it also allows men like your father to make a buck."

"Well, thank you for being honest."

"That's what I'm here for." Chris offered his arm, and they walked to their table together.

CHAPTER TWENTY-ONE

Jamie woke up with a beam of light shining in his eyes. Then it disappeared, leaving him blinded in the pitch-black dormitory. Then several pairs of hands grasped his limbs. They yanked him off the top bunk and he fell to the ground, crying out in pain. His attackers retaliated with kicks to his stomach.

Terrified, he fought back. He even screamed for help, but no one came. Only a couple of quivering chants in the distance. "Mordecai is great. Mordecai is good."

The attackers—he couldn't tell how many—bound him tightly with rope and dragged him through the rows of beds. They finally threw him into the dimly lit bathroom and tied him to a steel column. They left, only to return minutes later with someone else.

In the ambient light, Jamie couldn't make out the person's identity, but he guessed. "Eddie?"

"Yeah. What's happening?"

"I don't know."

"Shut up and listen." Saul's voice shot through the bathroom. Jamie looked up and saw three people. He figured Gideon and Obadiah were at Saul's side. Other beams of light popped on throughout the bathroom and Jamie realized there were more than just three people. There were at least ten people there. They looked like goons. Saul walked around the room, casting shadows that moved up and down the walls.

"Esrom and Roboam," he began. "God was angered by your behavior. So was Mordecai."

The desire to answer surged up in Jamie, but he resisted. Saul looked demented. Possessed. He knelt down next to Jamie. "You need to learn proper reverence to God." When Jamie didn't react, Saul grabbed his head and shook it up and down violently.

Pain from the jerks swept through Jamie. He quietly answered, "Yes. I need to learn reverence."

"That's better." Saul let his head fall onto his chest. "But now I face a dilemma. Which method of convincing will work best on you, physical threats or emotional ones? Or perhaps we should use punishments with Biblical significance. Christians have used many methods to rehabilitate sinners."

"How about castration?" Gideon offered.

"Yeah," Obadiah said. "Nothing works better on pretty boys than threatening to cut off their balls."

Saul moved closer to Jamie. "I like that idea. The Bible is filled with eunuchs." His spit sprayed Jamie's face. "But we have to be careful. We wouldn't want to spread discord among the Faithfuls, would we?" He looked over to his goons.

"How do we do that?" Obadiah asked.

"We don't. We let the Faithfuls do it for us. It's still cold inside the dormitories, isn't it, Gideon?"

"Yeah. We turned off the boilers long ago."

"Good." Saul stood and brushed the dirt off his knees. "Let's gather the Faithfuls and meet in the square."

Gideon and Obadiah left to rouse the Faithfuls from their bunks while Saul and the rest of the goons hauled Jamie and Eddie into the square. It didn't take long for them to gather.

Saul took on the posture of a preacher as he addressed the crowd. "Unfortunately, we had a disturbing incident that needs to be rectified," he said, drawing out his vowels. "Two Faithfuls have engaged in unclean activities. We need to make sure their sinful behavior is stopped."

The Faithfuls looked around for the sinners. Someone in back yelled, "Who are they?"

"I refuse to place blame," Saul continued, looking directly at Jamie and Eddie. "That would not be Christlike. But it is my duty to rectify their behavior. Starting tonight, *all Faithfuls* must sleep with their hands outside the blankets."

Another person asked, "And everyone gets punished for the sins of just of two Faithfuls?"

"That's not fair," Grandpa Swanson complained. "It gets cold at night. Our fingers will get frostbite."

"I'm sorry, but everyone must pay for the sins of the few." Saul took a flower from his pocket, put it to his nose, took a long whiff, and dropped it on the ground. Jamie understood the significance. Saul was acting under direct orders from Mordecai.

The Faithfuls spontaneously chanted, "Mordecai is great. Mordecai is good."

CHAPTER TWENTY-TWO

Holy Wednesday, early morning

When Saul finished his announcement, everyone returned to the dormitories. Obadiah grabbed Eddie and escorted him back with the rest of the Faithfuls while Gideon took hold of Jamie.

"I'll go without a problem," Jamie said, shaking off Gideon's grasp. He began walking. When he arrived at his bunk, he crawled in and closed his eyes. He was awake, though, shivering. His hands were frozen and his heart pounding. He couldn't make sense of Saul's latest actions. He felt defeated, and the grumbling from the Faithfuls around him didn't help. They complained about how Saul was punishing the innocent along with the guilty. They even made threats about what they'd do if they ever discovered the identity of the sinners in their midst.

In the distance, those damn gunshots started in the same location as before, but with much more frequency. Jamie peeked through a hole in the wall and saw nothing but tree branches and black sky.

Everything's a mess now. We're being watched and I still don't know who sent us the package. Or why. Jamie knew the secret to the package's message had to be obvious, he just didn't know where to look. Now that he was number one on Saul's special attention list, any unusual activity would arouse even more suspicion. But they had to start looking for clues, no matter what. Time was running out and all he could do was stay in his bunk, worrying and waiting.

About an hour later, the majority of Faithfuls began snoring and Jamie decided time for action had come. He delicately got out of his bunk and snuck through the shadows to Eddie's dormitory.

Making it to Eddie was easy compared to waking him. Jamie worried that he'd scream if he was startled. Eddie's hands were obediently outside his blanket, so Jamie warmed his own hands before lovingly massaging Eddie's arms. Nothing happened. Jamie stuck his hand under the blanket and gently rubbed Eddie's legs. He instantly sat up with a look of terror on his face.

Jamie covered Eddie's mouth quickly. "Shh. It's me," he whispered. "We have to be quiet."

"You scared me half to death."

Jamie didn't apologize. "We have to hunt for clues."

"Now? Wouldn't it be less suspicious if we did it in the morning?"

"Saul hasn't had time to fortify his sentries. Right now, there are only a couple of guards in the whole compound. In the morning, every Faithful will be awake and watching us. Our chances are better now."

Eddie nodded and got out of his bunk. Jamie propped up the blanket to make it look like he was still sleeping.

"What about the hands?" Eddie asked.

"They'd realize you weren't inside the bunk before they noticed your hands. Let's get going."

However, in the open air Jamie realized how little of the Brethren's compound they'd actually seen. They had to visit each building and determine if anything suspicious was happening there. If a building looked suspect, they'd take a chance and go inside to investigate. Jamie even stole a pencil and a piece of papyrus to make notes.

"If we keep alert, we'll find clues," Jamie told Eddie.

"But what if we get caught?"

"We'll say we were trying to find the stables."

"Why would we do that?" Eddie asked.

"Because we wanted to get an early start *mucking*."

"Great. And they'll probably say, 'muck you, too.'"

Jamie smiled and started surveying the area. For a moment, everything was quiet. Then more gunshots rang out in the distance.

"What the hell was that?" Eddie asked.

"Gunshots. That's another thing we have to find out about." He gave Eddie a comforting pat and began surveying.

"And we can't forget noting all the possible hiding places." Jamie gave him a questioning look. "Just in case."

The compound was laid out in a big circle, with the public square filling the nucleus. On one side were the dormitories, mess hall, and a large, enclosed root cellar. On the other side of the circle were the Disciples' living quarters, along with an old clapboard church and the stables. Jamie decided to leave that building for last so they could hide their map somewhere inside, buried in the hay.

But Jamie was still confused. He looked over the compound and asked, "If this is the entire place, aren't a lot of necessary things missing?"

"Yeah. Like, where are Mordecai and Saul's living quarters? And where are the SUVs parked?"

Jamie took a deep breath. "Those places are probably hidden, which makes them even more important to find." He looked at the dirt below him. Finally, he spotted tire tracks that looked like they came from an SUV. He grabbed Eddie's arm and followed the tracks, which led them past the chapel, through thickets and various muck until they encountered a row of spruce trees.

"Too uniform to have grown naturally," Eddie said. Jamie agreed. The trees had probably been planted to help hide something. He looked at the SUV tracks, which ran parallel with the trees. Instead of taking the long route around the row, he and

Eddie climbed through the spruces. On the other side was a huge asphalt parking lot, filled with the monster SUVs. A tall chain-link fence ran around the perimeter, and the gate had a motion detector attached to it. Jamie figured it connected to the halogen lights affixed at the top of the fence.

He put his hand in front of Eddie, stopping him from going closer. "We couldn't get inside anyway," he said, pointing to an electronic lock on the gate. "Our best bet is to look over there." He pointed to several brick buildings. They were two stories high. Dim lights illuminated the doors and, as with the parking lot, electronic locks prevented unwanted visitors.

That didn't surprise Jamie—what shocked him was there weren't any windows in the buildings, no way to look in or out. He figured it was probably for protection. Light, however, escaped from the thresholds of the entry doors, so he didn't try going inside. Instead, they circled the building and found an iron fire-escape ladder fastened to a back wall. They climbed to the rooftop and found another surprise: a parabolic antenna—a huge satellite dish colored to blend in with the roof. Jamie doubted it was painted that way for aesthetic reasons. More likely Mordecai wanted to minimize the chances of an airplane pilot spotting it while flying over.

The sun would rise in a couple of hours, so Jamie put his hand on Eddie's shoulder. "We'd better get to the stables before we run out of time."

They ran to the barn. When Jamie saw its condition, all he could think was *holy shit*. The place hadn't been cleaned in months. Animal dung was everywhere, and the smell was even worse than the stench that came from the dormitory bathrooms. Several scabby workhorses inhabited the stalls. They were obviously overworked and abused. They probably hadn't been groomed in weeks.

"Poor things," Jamie said. "Let's find some equipment and at least brush their manes."

"Not yet," Eddie told him. "There's something more important for you to look at."

Jamie turned around and saw the back end of the stables, where a beautiful, perfectly groomed white horse whinnied. He gravitated to it and stroked its mane. "Isn't she beautiful? Do you know what kind she is?"

"He's a stallion," Eddie corrected, and started searching the rest of the stables. "And he looks like an Arabian. They're one of the oldest warhorses and have been around for over forty-five hundred years. But stallions can be pretty aggressive. I wonder why they just didn't buy a mare instead."

"Stop being so sexist." Jamie examined the stallion, continuing his loving strokes. When he reached the animal's hindquarters, he found an oddity. Parts of the horse were painted white. Jamie touched the coloring, and it stayed on his hands. The horse had spots of brown in it. Jamie couldn't figure it out.

"Jamie, you've got to see this," Eddie interrupted. Jamie looked up and saw Eddie by the side of a veterinary cabinet. Inside appeared to be bottles and boxes of medications and such.

"Why doesn't Mordecai heal the animals himself?" Jamie asked.

"Probably because livestock is too expensive to lose," Eddie answered. Then he held another box out.

"What is it?" Jamie asked.

Eddie read from the bottle. "It's called Horse-Safe Dye for Manes, Tails, and Body."

"What color?" Jamie asked.

"Pure White."

Jamie ran to Eddie and examined the bottle.

"Why would Mordecai dye the stallion's hair?" Eddie asked. "It doesn't make sense."

"I know," Jamie answered. "Nothing makes sense around here."

"I'm getting scared, Jamie."

Jamie embraced Eddie tightly. Then he looked into his face and kissed him. Jamie was scared, too, and he hoped to alleviate that growing feeling in the pit of his stomach.

But it didn't help. A sudden, muffled noise came from the back.

CHAPTER TWENTY-THREE

Jamie's stomach tensed when he heard the noise a few stalls away. In his mind, he ran through a list of the sound's possible source. It wasn't mechanical, and he thought it was too human-like to be the white mare or the workhorses, so it had to be human. He wondered how long that human had been following them, and what he'd seen.

"Don't say a word," Jamie whispered. "We've got to back away from each other, but we gotta act casual doing it."

"Huh?" Eddie looked confused.

"Somebody's watching us."

"Oh." Eddie slowly backed up in the most artificial way possible. Each movement looked exaggerated. Fake. Jamie gave a big yawn. He stretched his arms and turned his back away from Eddie. He covertly scanned the stables, searching for the source. He didn't see anything, so he turned back and mouthed, *Stay here.*

In a voice twice as loud as normal, he announced, "Well, time to muck the stalls." It was the only thing he could think of to say. He grabbed his pitchfork and marched casually to where he thought the noise had come from.

But when he got there, he saw only hay. In the corner was an even bigger mound of the stuff. Moving up and down, like it was breathing. He crept to the undulating pile and gave it a stab with his fork.

The pile yelped.

"All right, slowly walk out of there."

The hay mound started moving and Peter crawled out. He looked more frightened than Jamie felt.

"What the hell were you doing in there?"

"Nothing."

"How long have you been there, doing nothing?"

"The whole time. I woke up and saw you and Eddie running around the square. I followed you guys."

"Did anyone see you?"

"I don't think so."

"Then how much of us did you see?"

Peter hesitated. "I saw you kissing."

"Shit."

"Are you guys *that way?*"

"What the hell are you talking about?" Jamie yelled. "Say what you mean."

"You know," Peter stammered. "Are you?"

"Are you're asking if Eddie and I are gay? Well, the answer is yes. We're queer." Jamie stuck his pitchfork into the ground. He looked at Peter's face and wondered if his innocence was for real. If Peter were really that naïve, Jamie didn't know how to handle the situation.

"I thought so," Peter said. "But I'm not that way, you know."

Jamie realized Peter wasn't concerned about their sexuality, but his own. "Eddie and I aren't judging you," he said. "You'd still be cool whether you liked boys or girls. Or both. It doesn't matter to us."

"I told you I'm not that way. I'm not."

Jamie's instinct was to comfort Peter, but then he thought, *What if I'm wrong?* It was possible he was putting on an act. But he was obviously distraught and didn't have anyone to confide in. Jamie told him, "I understand your fears."

Peter seemed to let down his guard. "I went to our family priest and asked him to help me."

"Did he help?"

"No. He told me God's perfect and doesn't create disease. Only Satan does that. And since being gay was my choice, my sickness, I'd have to fix the problem by myself."

Jamie knelt next to him. "So, what did you do?"

"I prayed at lot."

"Did it help?"

"No, I'm still…" Peter looked up at Jamie. "But I don't want to be."

Jamie didn't know what to say. He put his arms around Peter.

"And then the priest told my father about me, and he got angry. He said that I couldn't be his son."

"That must have hurt."

"I thought I'd die when I heard him say that. I should have died, you know."

"Why do you say that?"

"Because I tried to kill myself, more than once. Get everything over with. But I wasn't enough of a man to even do that right. That's why I came here. Mordecai will cure me."

"He can't cure you, Peter."

"Why can't he?"

"Because being gay isn't an illness or even a disorder. It's an essential part of your being. Your soul. Trying to live without a soul can only hurt you."

Eddie knelt next to them. "You know, Peter, we once had a friend who tried to change his sexuality. His parents enrolled him into conversion therapy."

"What happened?"

"We don't know. He ran away a couple years ago, and we lost contact. But I do know Jamie's right. An organization that promises to convert gays succeeds at only one thing: They make dysfunctional, closeted human beings. Don't let anybody do that to you."

"But I've got to change or I'll be all alone, and where would I go?"

"There will always be a place for you in this world," Jamie said. "There's a place for all of us. But I hope you know that place isn't here, at the Brethren."

Peter nodded and wiped away the tears. He hugged Jamie and Eddie tightly. Jamie wondered if he'd ever let go. Jamie told Peter to go back to the dormitories and pretend this never happened.

"Why?" Peter asked.

"Because around here, if you're not straight, you're going to be dead."

Chapter Twenty-four

Mordecai's eyes darted to the clock on his computer's desktop. Just after five in the morning. He hadn't been to sleep yet. It felt like he hadn't slept for days, yet he was exhilarated. He could see his years of planning and hard work finally paying off.

The Disciples' exercises had to be over and Sharar would be coming by to give him his daily briefing. In preparation, he powered off his computer and locked up its hardware. It wasn't that he didn't trust Sharar, but there were still too many loose ends with the mission. He couldn't chance anything.

But thank goodness things are going as planned here at the Brethren. He still had doubts about Ground Zero, though. Communication with his mole had always been spotty. Yet hours ago, Mordecai got a transmission saying the mole had an opportunity to infiltrate the enemy's camp and needed several of the Disciples.

Mordecai worried the request might be a setup. His mole could be a double agent. That seemed unlikely, though. Mordecai's sources said he was the best money could buy. But still—a man who could be bought could easily sell himself to the other side.

The door to his office banged. It had to be Sharar. The man never accepted his place. *Sharar always wants more, even if it belongs to me. Probably thinks I should leave the door unlocked just for him.*

If Sharar weren't so good, Mordecai would have left him long ago. Sharar was an abomination, yet also the closest thing to a friend he had. In fact, he almost liked the guy. Sharar was intelligent and never let money get in the way of achieving his goals.

If only he could control those *urges*.

Mordecai punched the code into the security system. The reinforced steel door obliged. Sharar stepped in and waited. A power play, no doubt. Sharar was waiting for him to shut the door, so Mordecai ordered, "Close the door."

"It's a little stuffy in here," Sharar replied. "Thought we could use some fresh air."

Sharar didn't move, and neither did Mordecai. After twenty seconds, the security system timed out and the doors automatically shut, making a loud clank as they locked.

Mordecai thought every bad word imaginable, but said, "How did things go at the field exercises?" It wasn't small talk; he would never engage in a conversation that wasn't necessary. The field exercises were the only thing that mattered right now.

"The mission will go fine, if that's what you're worried about." Sharar walked around Mordecai's office as if he owned it. He picked up a bottle of ink and started examining it.

Mordecai snatched the bottle from his hands. "So you'll be ready for Easter?"

"I told you, the mission will be a success. We've done it before."

"But we've only done it with one gunman and one target." Mordecai slammed the bottle on the table and ink slopped over the side.

Sharar obediently took out his handkerchief and blotted up the mess. "Then we'll continue our field exercises, if you insist."

"I do insist," Mordecai said. Then he paused, a little unsure how Sharar would react next. "But there's been a slight change of plans."

Sharar looked angry. "What change of plans?"

"Our mole at Ground Zero requested we send him several of our Disciples."

"What the hell for?"

"Don't curse, Sharar."

"I'll swear if I want to. We have been planning this mission for two years, and we've always included all twelve disciples in those plans. Now, one week before D-Day, you ask me to give up some of my men."

"The mole will put them to good use at the site, so there's no debate on this matter. So you'll do it?"

"Do I have a choice?"

"No. But don't worry—as long as you're prepared."

"I'm not worried about my side of this mission," Sharar said, putting the stopper back on the ink bottle. "But I am worried about how prepared your side is." He tossed the bottle to Mordecai without warning.

He caught it, and tried to control his temper. He couldn't blow up at Sharar, not this close to the mission. "I don't know what you're implying."

"Well, you must be nervous. A week before the mission, and you find it necessary to give away *my* men, all the while you gather more Faithfuls *for your side*."

"Bringing in new Faithfuls wasn't for the mission. It's our spiritual duty."

"Oh, right. I forgot." Sharar walked to the liquor cabinet and helped himself to the wine. "When are you gonna start stocking the good stuff? Something harder than communion piss?"

Sharar's blasphemy didn't shock Mordecai, but he still hated him for it. Mordecai stood firm and said, "I'll stock better liquor when you stop fucking boys."

Sharar scowled at him in return. But Mordecai knew Sharar had reason to be self-assured. Still in his thirties, he was tall, muscular, and good-looking. He used his natural sex appeal to control his Disciples, gay and straight. They adored him, but the feeling wasn't mutual. It was dominating them that appealed to Sharar. Mordecai admired that, and envied him, too.

Sharar lifted his glass to eye level and swirled the wine inside before gulping it down. "I honestly thought you'd be more concerned with your part of the mission. This is what you dreamed about since you got expelled from seminary, isn't it?"

Mordecai felt his control of the situation slipping out of reach. He couldn't let that happen. "If I recall, Sharar, we were both expelled from seminary."

Sharar licked his finger and drew a point for Mordecai in the air. "Of course, I was only expelled from one institution of higher learning. How many did you get kicked out of?"

"God has appointed me to be by his side," Mordecai told him. "So what I've achieved at the Brethren speaks louder than any academic record."

"*Mea culpa.*" Sharar bowed slightly. "Remember when you changed our names to Mordecai and Sharar?"

"I do. What about it?"

"Well, I don't remember what our names were before that."

"Our prior names don't matter, Sharar. What matters is that you realize I'm the brains of this operation. You're only the brawn."

"Oh, I know that. And I hope you know if your mission fails, you'll be considered one of Christianity's biggest villains."

"But I won't fail. And the world will enter into a new era. Today the world identifies its epochs of time by the designations BC and AD. But after Easter Sunday, everything changes." Mordecai grabbed Sharar's wine and threw it against the wall. "After Easter, the world will realize my brilliance. They'll fall to their knees in gratitude. They'll worship me, and they'll designate the modern age as RM. The Rèalm of Mordecai."

Sharar raised his empty hand as a toast. "Well then, here's to the Realm of Mordecai."

CHAPTER TWENTY-FIVE

A nother call came in as Ellen pressed the fourth digit of Jamie's phone number. She quickly answered, praying it was Jamie. It wasn't—it was Chris, calling to say he'd pick her up in an hour. She told him she'd be ready and hung up.

She tried to call Jamie again, still hoping it had been poor reception that kept him from answering the other times. Her call immediately went to voicemail, and she feared the reason was something more dangerous. Frantic, she called the phone company to report a problem. The man who answered took her information, but he refused to do anything else since it wasn't her account. She contemplated calling the police. It had only been two and half days since she and Jamie last talked. Aggravating? Yes. Proof of a crime? No.

Chris was the ideal person to pass the time with. He seemed to understand her and care about her investigation. She went down to the lobby to wait. He drove up, and they left to visit some of Boston's poorest neighborhoods.

"Rhodes's charity efforts really shine at the community centers," Chris said. "Free meals for seniors, tutoring for students, job counseling for the unemployed. All this underwritten by your father." Ellen thought he sounded like a press release. In fact, the center they visited looked like a photo op. The Rhodes Petroleum logo was all over the center—painted on signs and printed on the center's brochures.

I'm glad Daddy's generosity helps people. I just wish he would help Jamie and Eddie, too.

She decided to fully confide in Chris. "My best friends went to that cult in the Adirondack Mountains. I haven't heard from them, and I'm afraid something might have happened."

Chris looked at her intently. "And you're afraid that the cult might be the reason you haven't heard from them?"

Ellen nodded. "Jamie promised to keep in touch, but he doesn't answer my calls."

"Well, I'm not sure you can do anything about it. It's sad, but I've heard people who get messed up in cults often cut off contact with their family and friends."

Ellen got frustrated. "Jamie wasn't joining the cult. He and Eddie got a message about the cult and were trying to infiltrate it. You see, Jamie sees himself as an amateur spy. A gay 007. He and his husband went to the Adirondack Mountains to investigate the Brethren. He asked me to go to Boston and see if there might be a connection with my father's company."

Chris thought a moment. "Would you like me to send e-mails to everyone at the Boston branch asking if they know anything about the Brethren?"

"That would be good idea." If the connection between the Brethren and Rhodes Petroleum was through an employee, the e-mail would tip him off that people were on to him. But she couldn't think of a better alternative, so it was worth taking the chance.

Chris put the car into gear and started driving. But he didn't get on the freeway, and he didn't go to Dedham, either. He went north, to Faneuil Hall Marketplace, outside Boston's government district, and parked.

"Why did we come here?" Ellen asked. "It's a tourist spot."

"They have free Wi-Fi." Chris got out his laptop and started setting it up. "There's always a lot of people in the area, so the Internet access is practically anonymous. With so many people surfing at the same time, it would be almost impossible to discern who's doing what online. It's one of the few public places Rhodes allows employees to use the Internet, as long as they follow a long list of security protocols."

"Ah," she said, not quite understanding it all. "Can I do anything?"

"Yeah. Open the glove box and get my dongle."

"Your what?" She looked over at Chris, but he had a serious look on his face.

"My dongle." This time he smiled.

"Okay, I'll bite," she said. "What's a dongle? It sounds dirty."

"I wouldn't be that lucky. It's a little box that you plug into your computer for safe computing."

"Oh, more boring stuff."

"Yeah. Your father is paranoid about cyber security. The dongle makes sure that the person accessing the Rhodes Petroleum private network is on a sanctioned computer. But since there are so many other ways to crack into a system, it hardly seems worth it."

"Oh," Ellen said, like she understood him. She opened the glove box and found two of those little boxes. They looked almost identical. She held them up. "So, which one is it?"

"This one," he said.

Ellen held up the other box. "Then what's this one for?"

"That one allows me to surf porn sites without being identified." He arched his eyebrows and winked.

"Oh, I'm sure. What's it really for?"

He looked into her eyes. "If I told you all my secrets, they wouldn't be secrets."

"I guess you're right," she said, and watched Chris compose his e-mail:

Attention: If anyone has information regarding the Brethren, please contact me ASAP. A person of interest to Rhodes Petroleum might be involved with them. The

Brethren is a conservative Christian denomination, adhering to a strict interpretation of the Bible.

Ellen almost cringed. The last sentence nearly quoted verbatim the web page Jamie had found on his smartphone. She wondered if Chris had been doing his own research.

And if so, why?

DEADLY CULT

CHAPTER TWENTY-SIX

B arely midmorning and Mordecai had already encountered
problems. A cop from the Adirondack State Park came to
visit, saying he wanted to show "the head priest" something. He
wouldn't say what it was, so Mordecai guessed what kind of civil
servant he was—one on the take.

*Government peons always want their payoff. And if that's
the case, I want to make sure I get my money's worth. I already
bought off half the elected officials in the county, what are a few
more civil servants?*

He told Saul to bring the cop to the chapel. Mordecai didn't
want the Faithfuls to see a law officer traipsing through the
compound, but it was better than meeting him in his office. There
was too much confidential information there. Besides, he could
always take care of a pesky Faithful if he needed to.

Or a dirty cop, for that matter.

Mordecai stood with his back to the altar and adjusted his
sash. Holding a Bible in one hand, he lifted the other hand up to
God. An overdone pose, perhaps, but he liked it anyway. He gave
Saul the go-ahead and waited for the state's civil servant—soon
to be the Brethren's servant—to enter. Saul ushered him inside.
Overweight, he looked stupid dressed in the predictable uniform
of drab khakis, a too-short olive jacket, and the obligatory wide-
brimmed hat with chin strap.

"Show some respect," Mordecai yelled. "Remove your hat. This is the Lord's house."

The officer complied. "Are you the head priest here?"

"Well, I'm the spiritual leader," Mordecai replied. "We don't believe in the hierarchy of the priesthood or seminaries. Knowledge of God and his commandments should be common knowledge."

Mordecai took a seat in the first pew and let the sheriff stand. "So, what did you come here for?"

The man scratched his head.

"Speak up and speak fast, Officer, I'm busy saving souls. What are you busy at? Not much, by the looks of it."

The officer gave him a dirty look. "An abandoned car was found on state property just a couple of miles from here. Inside the glove box was this." He produced a tattered envelope from inside his jacket. "Thought you might want to know what's in it."

"And why would I be interested in something like that?"

"Well, if you're not, I can go back to the department and file it away. It would probably sit there for a couple of hours before somebody would open it up. But then it would be too late for you to do anything about."

"Okay, let's see what you think I might be interested in." Mordecai reached for the envelope, but the cop pulled it away.

"Sorry, Mr. Spiritual Leader. I went to great expense coming here, even bent a few rules. I figure the contents of this envelope might be worth something, especially to you."

"How much?" Mordecai asked.

"At least five thousand bucks."

"How do I know it's worth five grand if I don't know what the contents are?"

"I guess you'll have to take my word for it. Think of it as a leap of faith."

Mordecai paused, pretending he was considering the proposition, and nodded to Saul. "Give the man his thirty pieces of silver."

The cop pulled back the envelope. "I said the price was five thousand bucks."

"Sorry, Officer, a figure of speech. Saul, give the man ten thousand dollars." Mordecai gave the visitor a wide smile. "Think of the extra money as payment for services not yet rendered."

Saul dug into his pocket and handed the money over. The officer looked alarmed, but he took the payment and gave Saul the envelope.

"Wonderful." Mordecai clapped his hands and took possession of the information. "Saul, since our business is finished with this good man, will you be kind enough to escort him outside?"

"Certainly." Saul took the officer by the elbow and led him to the door.

"One more thing," Mordecai interjected before they left. "This entire transaction has been video recorded, so don't get the idea that you can renegotiate our terms in the future." He stepped closer, about six inches from the officer's face. "Bribing a public official is against the law, but so is accepting a bribe. Your bosses would probably be very angry if they ever found out."

A worried look spread over the officer's face, but Saul dragged him away before he could say anything.

When Mordecai was alone, he opened the envelope and extracted a folded piece of paper. Two gold rings and two driver's licenses fell out. Examining the contents, he started laughing. *Jamie Bradford and Eddie Delgado. And by the looks of these rings, they're legally married. They're making this so easy for me it's almost amusing.*

Then Mordecai read the note and he didn't think they were funny any longer.

To whom it may concern: This vehicle is not abandoned. We came to the Adirondacks with hopes of tracking down the cult known as the Brethren. We have reason to believe

*that illegal and nefarious things are happening there.
Our friend Ellen Rhodes is working on leads in Boston.
If this note is found, please contact her immediately. We
plan on updating her every night about the situation
here. She will be your best source for information.*

The faggots were friends of Ellen Rhodes. Mordecai knew
who she was. She was Elden Rhodes's daughter, but he didn't
care. He just wanted to make sure she wouldn't screw up his
plans. And the only way to do that was to pretend he was Jamie
and convince her that everything was hunky-dory. He knew he
couldn't call her, but he could text her. He called Saul back. "Do
we still have the fairy's cell phone?"

"Yeah. I haven't had time to sell any of the phones yet.
Why?"

"Because when the time's right, I'll have to text this Ellen
Rhodes." Mordecai read the note again. He crumpled the paper
into a little ball and laughed hysterically. *Those queers aren't
only in danger. They're good as dead, along with Ellen Rhodes
and her wealthy father.*

CHAPTER TWENTY-SEVEN

Church bells clanged from the sound system, followed by a song of praise. Jamie and Eddie ran out of the stables to find out what the noise was for. The Faithfuls were running into the square. They lined up.

"Must be for Ash Wednesday service," Eddie said, and they joined the parade.

Inside, the organist pedaled away on an old-fashioned pump organ. He played a hymn Jamie didn't recognize. No one else must have, either. The Faithfuls hummed the tune anyway.

Saul entered with Obadiah, Gideon, and Peter behind him. They walked up the aisle and took their places by the altar. Peter had a forlorn look on his face, as if he'd been crying all day. He saw Jamie and Eddie, and his expression started to swing the other way. Jamie shook his head and turned away. He didn't like treating Peter so coldly, but he couldn't take any chances.

At least, not in front of everybody.

The organist stopped and the congregation stood. A group of men entered in a procession from the back. Jamie leaned over to a neighboring Faithful and asked who they were.

"Our saviors," the neighbor said. "The Disciples."

The first Disciple was drop-dead gorgeous. The others—none as hunky as the first—followed. Jamie recognized the fat man, Raamiah. He looked mean and ugly as ever.

When the Disciples took their seats, Jamie looked. He saw a young man standing in the back, about the same age as he and Eddie. The guy stood in the shadows, behind a column. He even hid his face. He'd obviously entered with the Disciples, but appeared much lower in rank.

Mordecai entered and the organist started pedaling again. He processed to the pulpit and began. "It's not easy being a follower of the Brethren. We must fight evil every day."

"Amen," Grandpa Swanson yelled.

"But we knew it was a difficult task. Didn't I tell you that? And have I ever lied to you?"

Someone cried out, "No, you've never lied."

"Not once!" yelled another.

"And I'm being truthful now. We've waited patiently for the Brethren's time to come. We've worked hard, toiling in anticipation. Never asking for anything in return, simply waiting for our reward in heaven."

"Alleluia," someone shouted. "Our time is coming!"

"No," Mordecai yelled. "The devil has taken our moment away. Sin has entered our home. There are two among us that threaten our very existence. They're vile, dirty, and spawned from the devil."

"Are they the ones Saul warned us about?" a woman yelled. "What did they do?"

"They engaged in perverted forms of sexual licentiousness. But I can't go into the details. It's too shameful." Mordecai closed his eyes and turned his head. It built up the suspense, and Jamie could practically see the hate seethe inside the Faithfuls.

Mordecai opened his eyes. "They are men who lie with men as they would with a woman."

The congregation gasped. Even Jamie was shocked. *Did Peter tell Mordecai about us? Could he be just as bad as they are?*

Mordecai cried, "Oh, the abomination!"

And Grandpa Swanson yelled out, "Who are the faggots?"

Mordecai left his pulpit and walked to Jamie and Eddie's pew. "I cannot reveal that information. At least not yet." He stood over them and looked down. "But I will ask the two sinners to stand up and confess their sins in front of the Brethren."

Jamie froze. Eddie, too.

Mordecai looked around the congregation. "I command the unrepentant sinners to reveal themselves. Now." He looked down at Jamie and Eddie again.

They said nothing. Mordecai pointed to a weasel-like man in the third row and asked, "Are you the vile one?"

The man shook his head.

"Then is it you, old man?"

"Heck no. I've got grandchildren," Grandpa replied. The congregation didn't laugh this time.

"Then we must be patient and wait for the sinners to confess of their own accord. But rest assured, truth and righteousness will triumph."

Jamie knew this was just a hint of things to come. Mordecai would divulge the transgressors' names at a more opportune time, when the Faithfuls' abhorrence to gays simmered at the boiling point.

The hate would boil over, and their lives would be in danger.

CHAPTER TWENTY-EIGHT

A fter the three-hour service, Jamie was dead tired. He avoided contact with the rest of the Faithfuls and lay down in his bunk. He tried to review the horrid events of the day, his hands outside of the blankets, of course.

Could Peter really have betrayed us? No matter who had told Mordecai, they still had to be careful. And Jamie still had to discover who was responsible for the shooting sprees. He was sure their mission depended upon that knowledge.

When the snores from his dorm mates became loud enough to cover up his movements, he slid down the bunk and ran to Eddie's dorm. Eddie was rubbing his legs. He'd gone days without his medicines.

Jamie suggested he sit out tonight's expedition. But Eddie whispered, "Like hell I will," and hobbled outside with him.

Jamie's plan was simple. He and Eddie would wait until they heard the guns, then follow the sound to where it was happening and scope it out. The best place to wait, Jamie said, was the main gate, hidden by the bushes.

Eddie agreed with the plan. "And it's not like you haven't rolled around in the bushes before."

Jamie snickered and started walking.

They hid when they reached the gate. Every so often, the links would give off a crackle as an insect hit the metal and was fried by the electricity surging through it. Several minutes later, Jamie started squirming.

"You got ants in your pants?" Eddie asked.

"No. It's just that all of a sudden, my butt itches."

Eddie looked down and gasped. "Do you know what poison ivy looks like?"

"Yeah. 'Leaves of three, let it be,' but that's for summer. It is barely spring. It's freezing out here."

"Jamie, poison ivy doesn't go away in the winter. Only the leaves do, that's why there's another part to the rhyme. 'Hairy vines, no friend of mine.'"

"Fuck!" Jamie stood up and pulled down his linen pants. Red splotches began appearing on his ass. He couldn't help scratching.

Eddie pushed his hands away. "That'll only make it worse. You told me that yourself."

"What a great pair we are. You rubbing your flea-bitten stomach and me playing with my butt like a monkey in the zoo."

Eddie grinned, then pointed to a nearby tree. "May I suggest we use that for our lookout instead?"

Jamie, sneaking a scratch, agreed. From that vantage point, they could see almost everything.

It didn't take long before they spotted several hyped-up SUVs pulling up to the Disciples' quarters. The doors to their log building burst open and out flew the hunky leader and his followers. But they weren't dressed in the Brethren's uniform of linen basics. Tonight they wore dress military uniforms, complete with M16 rifles hung over the shoulders.

Without saying a word, they climbed into the SUVs. Their movements looked practiced. The engines revved and the SUVs sped on their way to the gate.

"Good," Jamie said. "When they get here, we'll follow them."

"Well, I'll try," Eddie responded, pointing to his leg.

The vehicles approached and the electronic gate opened. "Must be an electronic monitor in the SUV," Jamie said. "Let's go for it before it's too late."

The last truck passed the gate, and it started to close. Jamie and Eddie jumped down from the tree. Saul and his goons appeared out of nowhere. They two-stepped toward them. Saul pointed his flashlight while the thugs pointed their guns.

"Halt," Saul said.

"Shit," Jamie said under his breath.

"Well, if it isn't Esrom and Roboam. What are you two doing out at this time of night? Or do I even want to know the details?"

Jamie thought fast. "No, sir. We were going on an evening constitutional." He poked Eddie in the stomach. "Right, Esrom?"

"I'm Roboam," Eddie whispered.

"Right. Roboam." Jamie turned to Saul and laughed. "So many names, it's hard to remember who begat whom."

"Cut the crap," Saul ordered. "You're lucky I don't ask one of my boys to shoot you for trying to escape. Guess it's my Christian love that's preventing me."

"You said escape. Does that mean we're prisoners?"

"I wouldn't say that, exactly. I'd prefer to think of it as voluntary servitude."

"You son of a—"

Luckily, Eddie cut Jamie off before he finished. "Thank you for your edification, Brother Saul."

"Our great Mordecai warned me this might happen. He suggested that hard labor would bring you two in line." Saul signaled his lackeys. They pounced on the boys, slapping handcuffs on them.

The boys were led to the side of the chapel, where two large mounds of rocks were piled twenty feet from each other. "We need to get this area cleaned up. So, Esrom, I want you to move the rocks from that pile and put them on the other mound."

"That doesn't seem so hard," Jamie said. "Roboam, why don't you rest while I tackle this?"

"Not so fast," Saul said. "Roboam will be moving the stones from the other mound and placing them onto your pile."

"But that doesn't make any sense. We'll just be moving stones back and forth."

"Get used to it. You'll both be doing it until your piles are gone. And that'll take a very long time."

"Will you at least take off our handcuffs?" Jamie asked.

"Do you really think I'm that stupid?" Saul sat down at the back steps of the chapel while his henchmen stood guard by each pile. "Get a move on. Time's a wastin'!"

Jamie and Eddie started moving their rock piles. Jamie let a smile escape. *At least we know one thing. Mordecai is up to something, and the Disciples are his militia.*

CHAPTER TWENTY-NINE

Zacchaeus stood at attention in the field, listening intently as Sharar addressed the Disciples. "Mordecai has requisitioned three of our men to be agents at Ground Zero." The Disciples grunted their displeasure. "I know, it's against common sense to revise our plans days before the assault, but I had no choice. At least we have Zacchaeus to help make up the number."

"But he's a plebe," Raamiah growled. "And barely a novice."

"Perhaps, but with his inexperience comes a desire to prove himself. And remember, 'the fewer men, the greater share of honor.'"

Zacchaeus looked at Sharar. He remembered the quote. It was from Shakespeare, *Henry V*.

"I don't give a rat's ass about honor," Raamiah growled. "But more cash ain't bad." He and the rest of the Disciples laughed.

"I'll look into the situation," Sharar said. "But now, since you have your newly revised assignments, let's begin."

A flurry of activity commenced. As the Disciples prepared for the tactical drills, Zacchaeus unloaded the SUVs. He tried to execute his movements with the expertise of a veteran soldier, divvying up the field vests and double-checking that the guns were loaded with ammunition. Then he stood next to Sharar and they examined the deserted field. It was no longer an agricultural area. Now it was a mockup of a city. Painted lines delineated where urban blocks began and ended. Scaffolding covered with plywood represented buildings. Propped-up ladders took the place of fire escapes.

Sharar blew his whistle and everyone lined up. Zacchaeus didn't know where to stand. He'd never attended the exercises before.

Everything was different for him now. *I'm special. One of Sharar's favorites. And with my help, the Disciples will be able to perform their maneuvers with precision.*

Sharar gathered the Disciples into a straight line and started their exercises with a round of calisthenics. Push-ups, sit-ups, and squat jumps. Then he ordered a two-mile run. Each Disciple was expected to finish in less than sixteen minutes. Raamiah failed the tests, of course. He was too fat, and his stomach kept getting in his way. Zacchaeus breezed through the exercises. He was young and fit. He took pride in his athletic abilities.

And he secretly took pleasure in Raamiah's failures.

Sharar reprimanded him quietly. "I know how you're feeling. But remember, Raamiah has other talents. For instance, he's our best long-range sniper."

"Forgive me, Disciple."

"No foul," Sharar said. Zacchaeus could have sworn Sharar had a glint in his eye. A glint for him, but he couldn't be sure. Sharar quickly gathered the Disciples for the tactical part of their exercises. They divided into small teams until only he and Zacchaeus were left.

"Which team shall I be with?" Zacchaeus asked.

"You won't be on a team. You'll be with me." Sharar brought his hand to Zacchaeus's cheek. "We'll be together." The gesture made Zacchaeus feel good.

The teams separated to conquer the mocked-up area. One team roamed the streets, shooting out the tires of the sawhorse vehicles to facilitate a rapid advance or an emergency withdrawal.

Another concentrated on sharpshooting, picking off mannequins dressed in black suits and purple robes. Raamiah's team practiced cover and concealment techniques. They found perches where they could hide in the building-like scaffolding. Only the tips of their rifles could be seen.

Sharar didn't join the exercises, however. He paid special attention to Zacchaeus. He showed him the finer points of firearms, taught him how to stand tall, his feet shoulder-length apart. How to aim his weapon without squinting and how to withstand the M16's fierce kickback.

When the exercises finished for the evening, Sharar put his arm around Zacchaeus's shoulder and gave him a manly embrace. "You did well today. You'll make a fine soldier."

Zacchaeus didn't want to smile. But he couldn't help it. Sharar had just given him a public sign of approval. He inched a little closer to Sharar and said, "Thank you, Disciple."

CHAPTER THIRTY

Maundy Thursday

Jamie got kicked in the ribs. It woke him instantly. He and Eddie had fallen asleep on their rock piles and Saul stood above them, hovering and seething. Saul ordered his goons to pull them upright. Peter was with them, but stood apart and did nothing. Jamie hoped he was having second thoughts about his allegiances. He called out to him for help, but Peter looked away.

The goons dragged them around to the square. Jamie tried to hit his abductors but was handcuffed, so the attempt was useless. Instead, he started kicking and biting while screaming as loudly as he could. Eddie joined in. It only made Saul angrier, and he ordered them gagged.

As they passed the dormitory, the Faithfuls started watching the commotion from the windows and doorways, reciting, "Mordecai is great. Mordecai is good."

After several circles around the square, the goons led them to the chapel and dropped them by the pump organ. Mordecai stood by the altar, watching everything. "Saul, didn't I tell you the faggots were trouble?"

"You were right." Saul lowered his head.

"I'm always right. Now remove their gags." Mordecai walked over to them and knelt down. His face was inches from

Jamie's. Jamie forced back his revulsion. "Why do you reject the Brethren's ways?" he asked. "Don't you want to be part of us? Don't you want to feel the Brethren's love?"

"Not if your love discriminates."

"We don't discriminate." He got almost indignant. "We love the sinner. It's the sin we hate. That's why we want to turn you toward righteousness."

Jamie spat in Mordecai's face. Mordecai wiped his cheek and gave Jamie a hard strike with the back of his hand. "Okay, we know how the prissy one feels," he said, turning to Eddie. "What does the cripple think?"

Eddie told him. "Growing up, I loved going to Mass with my family. I felt that I belonged. But when I got older, I realized I was different."

"That you were an abomination."

"That I was gay. When I came out, my church tried to take God away from me."

"And rightly so, since you refused to repent. Refused to live a righteous life."

"But the tactic didn't work. I still believe in God. I just don't believe in that church anymore. And I don't believe in the Brethren, either."

An aura of satisfaction seemed to take over Mordecai, and he grinned. "So I'm supposed to feel sorry for you? Sorry for a sinner? No. If you refuse to accept righteousness, it will be beaten into you."

As if on cue, Saul's goons pulled out a vat filled with whitish water and slung two ropes over the rafters. They seized the boys, tying their cuffed wrists to the ropes. They pulled the boys up, making them stand on their toes.

Saul removed a whipping cane from the vat. It had to be four feet long and about half an inch thick. It dripped the thick, whitish liquid. Saul handed it to Mordecai, who ran his fingers over the switch. Caressed it. Felt its dampness. "Pull down their pants," he ordered.

The henchmen obeyed and started laughing. "The faggy one's got a rash all over his ass!"

"Really?" Mordecai's satisfaction turned into elation. "Well, God has already started the punishment that I must now finish."

The goons laughed some more and Mordecai held out the cane in front of the boys. "But you don't have to worry. We soaked the cane in brine to disinfect it."

Jamie knew soaking it in salt water made it more flexible, heavier, and it made the gashes hurt that much more.

Mordecai took his position and raised his weapon.

"Should we put the gags back in?" Saul asked.

"No. I want all the Faithfuls to hear them scream."

"We won't give you the pleasure," Jamie told him.

"We'll see about that." Mordecai shifted his position. "I'm going to start on the invalid first, so you'll have to wait. Watching him and anticipating the pain you'll soon feel."

Mordecai took a deep breath and hoisted the cane in the air. Jamie refused to look and turned away, but a goon grabbed his head and gave it a twist, forcing him to watch everything. Mordecai swung the cane onto Eddie's buttocks with a swift swipe. The cane whistled through the air until it made contact with a hard thwack. The pain must have been excruciating. Eddie winced, but he held the scream inside.

"Now it's your turn, faggot." Mordecai repositioned himself and lowered the staff onto Jamie's backside. Jamie felt the staff slice into his flesh. He felt the blood oozing from his splayed skin. He thought he was going to die, but he refused to cry, refused to scream.

Mordecai became enraged. He continued swinging, hitting harder with each strike. He swung ten times. Five lashes for each. Jamie looked up between lashes and saw Peter standing there. He was crying, yet did nothing to help them.

When Mordecai finished his punishment, the goons cut the ropes. Jamie and Eddie collapsed, but still refused to utter a sound.

CHAPTER THIRTY-ONE

When Mordecai finished, the goons made Jamie and Eddie put their underwear on over the still-bleeding welts. The fabric turned brownish red, but the goons didn't seem to care. They hauled them to the front steps of the dormitory and the Faithfuls scurried outside. Once they saw who it was, they averted their gaze.

Mordecai's voice boomed over the loudspeaker. "Take heed and beware. God has allowed me to reveal everything now. The two you see before you are the infidels. The faggots are our enemies."

The crowd gasped and Mordecai continued. "Let their crumpled presence be a warning to anyone who even thinks of defying the Brethren. Until these criminals repent and turn toward righteousness, they shall be shunned. They are no longer human. They are animals, and should be treated like beasts of burden."

The Faithfuls looked at each other, their eyes conveyed the fear in their hearts. One of the Faithfuls even started crying. He asked, "What should we do now?"

Saul looked up to heaven. "We work for the glory of Mordecai."

In unison, the Faithfuls recited, "Mordecai is great. Mordecai is good. Mordecai will redeem me of my sins."

"And this is how it should be," Saul told them. "Now, there's work to be done, and we should to tend to our chores."

As the Faithfuls walked away, Jamie and Eddie took each other's hands. It was the only kind of embrace they had the strength for. One of the goons, on his way out, stepped on their embrace. He ground his foot into their fingers.

❖

Later that afternoon, the church bells rang and woke Jamie. He and Eddie must have passed out from the pain, sprawled on the steps. Jamie's body ached. His welts throbbed, and his blood continued to ooze from the lacerations. He looked at Eddie and wanted to cry. Eddie was wincing in pain, too.

Saul stood above them. "This doesn't excuse you from evening chapel."

Jamie tried to stand, but his wobbly legs couldn't support him. "We have no clothes. It wouldn't show proper respect for the Brethren to attend in bloodied underwear."

"Here." Saul threw them a couple of pairs of tattered linen pants. "Put these on, and show your respect."

Using each other for support, the boys slowly pulled up their trousers and walked to chapel behind the rest of the Faithfuls. No one spoke to them. No one even looked at them. The Faithfuls who passed their way quickly moved on, acting like Jamie and Eddie weren't there.

When they entered the chapel, Saul made them sit in the back pew by themselves. He signaled the organist to start playing, and he and his goons processed up the aisle. Peter walked with them. He turned toward Jamie, but Saul gave him a thwack to the side of his head and he looked forward.

The organist stopped playing when the Disciples entered. Their leader came first, followed by Gideon, Raamiah, and the rest. Jamie remembered the young man hidden in the background. He turned to see if he could catch a glimpse. The young man entered, but stood hiding in the darkness.

Then Mordecai entered with his red sash flowing. He stepped

to the pulpit and began his sermon. "The wages of sin is death. But there are many kinds of death…"

Jamie sat in his pew, silent. He couldn't comprehend anything Mordecai said. The words were meaningless. After ten minutes of his blathering, Jamie turned around in an effort to identify the hiding young man. He succeeded, but didn't believe what he saw. He nudged Eddie. Eddie looked back, and his eyes met the young man's. Eddie recognized him, too. It was Andrew Caldwell, a good friend from Stratburgh University. Andy saw Eddie and turned away quickly.

Mordecai stopped his sermon and pointed to Jamie and Eddie. "This impertinence will not be tolerated, especially from sinners. Saul, deal with them after the service." Saul nodded and they faced front again. Mordecai resumed sermonizing.

But Jamie smiled. *The pieces are beginning to fit together. Andy sent us the package. It was his class ring. It was his cry for help.*

After the service, Mordecai instructed the Faithfuls to stay in their pews while Saul's goons punished the boys. This time, the goons focused on their faces, pummeling them until they were black and blue. Peter stood in the back, doing nothing. Jamie wasn't sure what side he was on, until another goon yelled, "It's your turn, Caleb. Can't be lily-livered forever."

Peter walked to the boys slowly, his face tight with fear. He raised his fist and lowered it onto Jamie without any force. "Harder," the goons taunted.

Peter lifted his fist again and swung, this time with unusual power, knocking Jamie onto Eddie's shoulder. Peter brought his hand to his mouth and blew on his fingers. The goons complimented him: "Attaboy, Caleb."

Peter smiled. He grabbed Jamie by the nape of his neck and pushed him aside. Then he smiled at Eddie and started hitting him, too. When Peter finished, the goons patted him on the back and cheered his behavior.

Jamie looked into the congregation and saw the Faithfuls

sitting in their pews. Some had fear on their faces. Others appeared relieved. Some were probably worried that faggots would continue to disrupt the order in their lives. Others were more likely relieved Mordecai's hate was now focused on the homosexuals, and they were safe from his harm for now.

When the time came for Jamie and Eddie to leave the chapel, they rose onto their wobbly feet. They gained their balance and ran past the Faithfuls as quickly as they could. Everyone was ignoring them, but Jamie didn't care. They made their way to Andy Caldwell. He and the head Disciple were almost to the doors of their quarters. Before they could enter, Eddie yelled, "Please, Andy. Stop."

The young man stopped, but didn't turn around.

Eddie continued. "You're Andrew Caldwell. We went to school together at Stratburgh University."

The young man looked at the head Disciple, who gave him permission to speak. He slowly turned around, but didn't look at Eddie. He looked at the ground instead. "I'm afraid you've mistaken me for someone else."

"Don't be ridiculous, Andy. We were roommates for two years."

"But I'm not Andy. The Andrew Caldwell you knew is dead. It is Zacchaeus who lives now, and it is Zacchaeus who will live forever more."

Zacchaeus ran inside. The Disciple followed him at a steady pace.

Jamie gave Eddie an apologetic glance. He knew Andy was scared, and nothing they could do would change the situation. Eddie shook his head in disbelief. "Why would Andy deny knowing us?"

Jamie wanted to comfort Eddie with a soft touch. Instead, he said, "Because the head disciple was right there and could hear everything Andy said."

"Then we've got to figure out a plan to rescue him and us. It's our only hope."

Jamie agreed, but there was another pressing matter. He heard a loud ruckus in the square and saw Saul and his goons advancing. They had scythes and sickles in their hands, but they didn't look like they were going to tend the fields. They wanted to tend to Jamie and Eddie.

The boys didn't give them the chance. They scurried away like field mice to their hiding places.

CHAPTER THIRTY-TWO

Jamie and Eddie lost Saul and his goons. They ended up hiding in several of the places they had noticed during their survey, but had to keep moving to avoid being caught. Their last refuge was the stable. It wasn't a good hiding place, but they needed to take care of their injuries.

Jamie lay on his stomach in the hay, next to the white mare. His buttocks still bled, still stung like a son of a bitch. Eddie carefully removed Jamie's pants and inspected the injuries. "We've got to clean our cuts before they become infected. And heaven knows what the poison ivy is doing to your blood right now." He spotted the cabinet they'd found earlier and began rummaging through the bottles inside.

"What did you find?"

"The perfect solution. Iodine spray." Eddie held up the bottle and started reading the label. "'Use on cattle and horses prior to surgical procedures such as castrating.'"

"Castrating?"

"I'm sure it's just to stop infection."

"But is it safe on humans?"

"Should be. The only thing it says here is…" Eddie started reading again. "'Caution is advised when treating near the teats or udders of dairy animals.'"

"That does it," Jamie objected. "No way in hell."

"All it means is it's safe for sensitive skin. Besides, you're a human and you don't have udders."

Jamie considered his options. He didn't have any. They were stuck, but he wasn't going to let Eddie have the last word. "Okay. But I want you to know my nuts are a lot more sensitive than anything a cow has."

Eddie laughed. "Look, after I spray your backside, you can spray mine. Is it a deal?"

But before Jamie could agree, Eddie spritzed the iodine all over Jamie's wounds.

"Now it's my turn to spray you." Jamie got up and helped Eddie lie down on the hay. He pulled away the fabric covering Eddie's bottom and aimed the bottle inches away. "Trust me, sweetie. This is going to hurt."

Jamie gave the bottle a good pump. Brownish-orange medicine coated Eddie's buttocks, and he started crying. Through the sniffles he said, "I should have helped Andy."

"And what would you do, sweetie? Andy's obviously mentally disturbed or else he wouldn't have sent us the package."

Eddie didn't listen to him. "Andy needed my help, and I did nothing."

"We're here, aren't we? We're doing all we can."

"I'm talking about two years ago. When his parents pulled him out of school and put him into conversion therapy. I did nothing."

"There wasn't anything you could have done." Jamie tried to put his arms around Eddie. He tried to comfort him. But Eddie refused his help, so he mentioned the one memory he knew they both hated the most. "Eddie, you couldn't have done anything for Andy because you were busy rescuing me from Stephen Antonelli, and also saving the lives of three sorority girls."

Eddie sat in a stupor. "I failed Andy then. We can't fail him now."

"I agree, but I don't know what else we can do."

"So we give up?"

"No," Jamie said. "We just need to proceed cautiously. We're in hiding, but Saul and his goons are going to find us pretty soon, so we've got to go on the offensive."

For the next hour, Jamie and Eddie planned and prepared their attack. When Jamie heard the Faithfuls going inside the dorms for the evening, he knew it was time. Taking a breath to gather his senses, he asked Eddie, "Think we can do this?"

"Andy needs us. So yeah, we can do this." Eddie slung a huge burlap bag over his shoulder and added, "This is heavy. And it smells, too."

"Well, horseshit stinks. And I lost count of how many horseshoes and boxes of nails we put in the bags."

"Me too," Eddie said.

Jamie slung his bag over his shoulder, and they left the barn. They followed the moon's shadows across the compound until they got to the main gate. More specifically, to the bushes where Jamie got infected with poison ivy. Wearing latex gloves they found in the cabinet, they carefully uprooted the ivy and added it to the horseshit and nails. Then they rigged the bags in the tree's branches. Rigging up a trip line across the path, they secured it to the bags in the branches.

Their work almost finished, they hid themselves below. Jamie threw stones into the electronic eye of the security alarm, and it blasted.

It didn't take long for Saul, his goons, and even Peter to come running. The trip line worked, and the bags opened, dumping several months' worth of rotting horseshit laced with nails, rocks, and poison ivy over Saul and his underlings.

"Damn," Saul yelled.

A goon cried, "It's horse manure!"

"And it itches, too," said another.

Then Peter dropped to his knees and screamed with pain. "Something hit my eye. I can't see." He touched his brow and blood got all over his hands.

Saul didn't bother tending to Peter. Instead, he took a closer look at the feces, rubbed it between his fingers, and gave it a whiff. "It's laced with poison ivy, damn it!" He slung it to the ground.

"Help me," Peter cried. "I can't see."

"Stop whining," Saul said. "We have to head for the showers. Since the security gate's still closed, they can't escape, anyway." Saul and his subordinates ran, leaving Peter on his knees, blinded.

Jamie and Eddie ran to help Peter. But Peter shooed them away. "It's too dangerous to help me. You've got to leave."

"But you're hurt," Jamie said.

"I'll be all right. But you won't be. They're going to kill you. Please, leave now."

Jamie knew Peter was right. "Okay, but we'll be back to get you." He and Eddie left Peter.

CHAPTER THIRTY-THREE

They hurried to the Disciples' quarters to rescue Andy. When they reached the door and Jamie put his hand to the knob, he stopped.

"What do you think the odds are that this building is rigged with more alarms than Fort Knox?"

"About a hundred to one," Eddie answered.

"And what would be a normal reaction if an alarm did go off?"

"Run like hell."

"Yeah," Jamie said. "So, are you thinking what I'm thinking?"

Eddie nodded and Jamie turned the knob. The door opened, but nothing happened. Just as they were about to sneak inside, an alarm went off and glaring lights bathed the quarters.

"Well, you were right." Jamie winked at Eddie and the two dove for cover behind two nearby Adirondack chairs.

They heard the head Disciple barking his orders. "Spread out evenly. Be sure to take the front and rear lots as well as the sides. Zacchaeus, you stay here and guard the interior."

Perfect, Jamie thought. After the Disciples left, they could get Andy by himself. Peeking through the slats of the chair, Jamie watched the disciples evacuate the lodge. They almost looked like firemen, but Jamie knew saving anyone was the furthest thought from their minds.

Jamie watched as the head Disciple left the area. "Well, here we go." He and Eddie entered the quarters.

Jamie gawked at the lavish interior. "Talk about chic."

The Disciples lived in luxury. Rustic yet refined, the interior looked like it had been imported from an expensive skiing chalet, with overstuffed easy chairs with oak accents and tea services on the occasional tables. But they couldn't waste time. They started searching for Andy.

They found him upstairs, sitting on a mat in the hallway. There was a yellowed pillow by his side. Obviously, this was Andy's sleeping place. He was far below the status of a Disciple.

Andy looked up at them. His hands were shaking, and so was his whole body. He stuttered, "Hello, Eddie. Jamie."

Eddie ran to his side. "Don't worry. We're here to save you."

"But I don't need to be saved."

Jamie couldn't believe his ears. "You sent us the note and the ring, didn't you?"

"Yes, I sent you that package."

"Why send us a message like that if you didn't want us to find you?"

"When I sent it, I didn't know what I wanted. But I do now. I don't want to be saved."

Jamie couldn't believe it. "You sent us that package yourself. Less than a week ago. What's changed since then?"

"Everything's changed. The package doesn't mean anything. Not anymore."

"I'm so sorry, Andy." Eddie couldn't keep from crying. "I'm sorry for everything that's happened to you."

Andy took Eddie's hand. "There's no reason to be sorry. I have a life at the Brethren. I can be happy here."

Eddie shook his head and whispered, "No."

"Please," Andy begged. "Don't take the Brethren away from me."

Andy wasn't capable of rational thought, but neither was Eddie at the moment. He was wrapped up in guilt, so it was up to Jamie.

"What kind of life do you have here, Andy?" Jamie made his voice harsh, severe, and masculine. "You're a lackey. You do what you're ordered to do. You've got nothing. You even sleep in a hallway."

"It's better than sleeping in the streets."

"What?" Eddie asked.

"I was on the streets when Sharar found me."

Eddie put arms around Andy. "If you were in trouble, why didn't you try to get some help?"

"I did. The homeless shelters were worse than the streets. In a back alley, I could defend myself, or at least run away. On a mission cot, I was ripe for the picking. When no one was looking, the other residents would beat me up. They searched my things looking for drugs. And when they didn't find any, they took what little money I had."

"Andy, how did this happen? You were at the Second Birth Treatment Center."

"The center kicked me out. Said I was an incorrigible homosexual. Beyond curing. They didn't want me anymore."

"I'm sorry, Andy. You never should have gone there. Being gay isn't a sickness."

"But I didn't want to be gay. So I begged the center for one more chance. I told them I'd do anything not to be a fag."

"What happened then?"

"My counselor agreed. He gave me another try. He even promised to cure me. If I gave myself to him, he'd show me how unsatisfying my life as a homosexual was."

"And how did he do that?"

"Each time we had a session, all I had to do was give him a blow job."

Eddie turned away.

"He called it aversion therapy and said it was based on scientific studies. He went through the treatment himself, and it cured him. He said all I had to do was associate my sexuality with something bad. Since he was fat and ugly, I figured it might work. He even smelled."

"This is all my fault," Eddie cried.

Andy's eyes were red, too. Snot dripped from his nose. He wiped it with his linen sleeve. "But then my counselor wanted more. He started fucking me at each session, until it happened."

"What happened?" Eddie asked the question, but it looked like he didn't want to hear the answer.

"Another therapist walked in on us while he was fucking me. My counselor blamed me. Said it was my fault. That I seduced him, or else he wouldn't have relapsed. They all believed his lies, and I was expelled."

"Then you should have called your parents, Andy."

"I did. They wouldn't take me back." Andy's hands shook badly. "I had no place to sleep. No money to buy food. I started turning tricks on the street. For five bucks, I'd show it to you. For ten you could touch it. Twenty bucks got you a blow job. And you could fuck me for fifty."

"Stop it," Eddie begged. "This is all my fault."

"No, it isn't." Andy put his hand on Eddie's arm, and he stopped shaking. "I never blamed you, Eddie. And I never stopped thinking about you, either."

Andy went to a nook in the hallway and retrieved his footlocker. Inside, carefully wrapped in white tissue, was memorabilia from Stratburgh University. Articles about the Sorority Maniac and the student heroes. There were magazine ads for Le Chateau.

"I kept everything, Eddie. I kept it for you."

Andy held out the package and Eddie took it. "Thank you."

"You're welcome." Andy added, "I loved you, Eddie. I still do."

Tears welled up in Eddie's eyes. "No, you don't love me. Your memory's clouded. You don't remember how you felt about me during school. We constantly fought, and every night you went cruising for guys."

"That's because I was scared. I was scared of my feelings for you."

Andy buried his head into Eddie's shoulder, and Eddie held on to his friend as if their lives depended on it. "Maybe we were both scared," Eddie said. "But every time you came home from the park or the highway rest stop, I was jealous."

"Of me?"

"No. I wasn't jealous of you, Andy. I was jealous of them, your tricks. They were with you, even if only for a brief time. You see, maybe I loved you, too."

"Those tricks didn't mean anything to me, Eddie."

"They had to mean something, because you kept going back. You kept ignoring the people who cared for you. Loved you. People like me."

Jamie tried to sink into the wall and disappear. He couldn't believe his husband was saying those things. He knew Andy and Eddie cared for each other. They were best friends. But that had to be the extent of their feelings—they didn't love each other, not like Eddie loved Jamie.

Andy took Eddie's hand and placed it on his chest. "My heart still longs for you. You can have me if you want."

"No." Eddie took his hand away. "That was a long time ago, Andy. I love Jamie."

"I understand." Andy looked over at Jamie and back to Eddie, nodding with resignation. "Then I hope you understand why I can't go with you. The Brethren gave me a life. A reason to live."

Eddie nodded and stood up. He kept looking at Andy, but he held out his hand to Jamie.

Jamie accepted his hand, and together they started walking out of the quarters. But Jamie stopped and turned around. He said with a stoic voice, "I know reliving the past hurts, Andy. It hurts all of us. But there's a few things you haven't told us yet. Things that might help us."

"What do you need to know?"

"Well, one thing you haven't told us is how you met the Disciples."

"I kept drifting, going from state to state. I finally ended up in California. West Hollywood. Vaseline Alley, they called it. That's where Sharar found me. He let me stay with the Disciples, and when they finished their tasks, they took me home. Here, to the Brethren."

"What were the Disciples doing in L.A.?"

Andy looked away and said, "They were performing God's work."

Andy was talking nonsense again. Jamie decided he was too conflicted to help them stop the Brethren. Their best course of action would be to leave Andy here. After they escaped, they could send him help.

"Then it's time to leave." Jamie took Eddie's hand. At the door, they came face-to-face with Sharar. He was holding a pistol.

"Do you really think I would let Zacchaeus guard the quarters? I'm not that stupid. You two have caused enough trouble."

Sharar did a front-snap kick into Eddie's bad leg and he fell to the ground. Jamie knelt by his side.

Andy screamed, "No." He rose and ran to Sharar with his arms raised. But Sharar was bigger and stronger. He lifted his arm, and with the backside of his hand, hit him. Andy fell to the ground, sobbing.

Sharar stood over Andy. "You pissant faggot. I'll be damned if I let you stand in my way."

Sharar gave Andy another kick. Then he grabbed Jamie and Eddie and hauled them out of there.

CHAPTER THIRTY-FOUR

Jamie didn't know where Sharar was taking them until he dumped them into the root cellar. Jamie realized it wasn't a cellar at all. It was it was dark, moldy dungeon. Eddie was by Jamie's side, but he chose not to speak. It was a familiar choice now. Jamie kept quiet, too, and the hours passed slowly.

Squeaking and scampering sounds came from the corner. Jamie figured the mice or the rats were checking them out. But it didn't matter. Jamie felt like a complete failure, a prissy little nobody.

After more time passed, he asked, "How's your leg, sweetie?"

Eddie surprised him. "I've had better days, but I'll survive."

"Good." He bit his lip. He didn't want to ask the next question, but had to know the answer. "Eddie, did you really love Andy?"

"Yes."

That was the answer Jamie had feared the most. "So was I a consolation prize?"

"A what?"

"You know, like a Kewpie doll? Did you love me because you couldn't have Andy?"

"Don't be ridiculous."

"That's not an answer, Eddie."

"That happened two years ago. Everything was different then. We didn't even date."

"I know. But you still haven't answered my question."

There was an agonizing pause. Jamie was afraid of what it meant, and held his breath.

"Yes. I loved Andy, but I fell in love with you."

"Thank you." Jamie reached for Eddie's hand and grasped it in the darkness. They held each other for several minutes without saying another word.

Eddie finally asked, "Can you answer a question for me?"

"Of course."

"What the hell is a Kewpie doll?"

Their laughter was cut short by the clanging of keys. A strip of light cut through the darkness as the door to the dungeon opened. Mordecai and Sharar walked in carrying a kerosene lantern. The light cast menacing, ominous shadows onto the walls.

"You boys are more trouble than you're worth," Mordecai said. "And all we're trying to do is give you the chance at salvation."

Jamie tried to squint past the light. All he could see were their outlines. "This is America, Mordecai. You can't lock us away just because you don't like the way we live our lives."

"I just did." Mordecai's laugh echoed through the chamber. "Besides, this isn't a dungeon. It's the Brethren's Spiritual Confinement Center."

"So you confine people's spirituality here?"

"If need be, yes."

"Well, you'll never be able to confine mine or Eddie's. So what are you going to do with us?"

"Nothing, until after Easter."

"What happens then?"

"I'll hand down your sentence. Lapidation. Being stoned to death."

Jamie held his breath.

"It's a biblical tradition. First, we select the rocks. Size is very important. They have to be small enough so the victim isn't killed with just one or two throws. Yet the rocks have to be large enough to be dangerous, and eventually lethal."

"Very ingenious," Jamie said.

"Then we'll bury you waist-deep. Your hands will be tied, too. That way, you can't escape."

"Figures."

"And then the Faithfuls will take turns pummeling you with their rocks. They'll like that."

"That's where you're wrong, Sharar. They have no reason to hate us."

"Hate doesn't need a reason. It just needs to be cultivated."

"No. People aren't murderers. They don't like to kill."

"And that's where you're wrong," Mordecai corrected. "People love to kill. What they don't like is experiencing the punishment if they're caught. But guilt is a funny concept. The more it's shared, the less it bothers people, and that's the great thing about stoning. It doesn't cast blame. Since the wounds are cumulative, no one particular throw can be proven to have actually caused the death. And everyone is innocent."

"And it's all for the glory of Mordecai," Jamie said sarcastically.

"You're absolutely right." He held up his arms to the sky. "Thanks be to me. And if things go well this Easter, I might broadcast your execution on national television. Now if you'll excuse us, I have some things to attend to."

Chapter Thirty-five

Ellen's cell phone rang and vibrated at the same time. Her heartbeat increased as she picked up the phone. The text message was from Jamie.

> *Girlfriend, I am extremely sorry for not getting back to you. I have decided to call off the investigation since nothing bad is happening here. Everyone is pretty chill. We will be going home soon. I will talk to you later. Sweetcakes.*

"Thank goodness he and Eddie are safe," she said to herself. "I knew that message had to be a joke. On papyrus paper? It was just too weird."

She looked at Jamie's text one more time. It was strange, too. It didn't look like a typical message from Jamie. The language was stilted, it didn't have any abbreviations or emoticons. *And* it was punctuated, which Jamie never did. And she'd never heard him use the word *chill* before.

She returned his text. *AYS CM 88, Ellen* In other words, *Are you serious? Call me! Hugs and kisses, Ellen*

She waited a long time, but didn't get the requested phone call or even another text. A list of possible scenarios ran through her mind when the second text came through: *Sorry, but I have got to go. My husband is calling me. Later, sweetcakes.*

She felt a little better, even though Jamie's response still didn't seem normal. *But I've got to allow the guys some slack. Being stuck inside an ultraconservative cult would probably change anyone. When they get back home, I'll deprogram them with Katy Perry songs.*

She plopped herself down on the couch, laughing. *Thank God my boys are okay.* Now was the perfect opportunity to forget about the investigation and get to know Chris on a personal level.

Criminy! She'd forgotten all about Chris. They had an appointment to meet at his place near the Boston Harbor. She checked the clock. She was late.

She programmed Chris's address into her Porsche's GPS. Hoping to save time by avoiding the sightseers, she sped down side streets rather than taking the main road. But when she got to his address, it wasn't an apartment or a condo. It was a posh hotel, even swankier than the company's corporate condos in Dedham.

She went inside the lobby, where the concierge said she was expected. A bellboy escorted her to the Independence Suite on the top floor, room 1212. When they got there, he even rang the doorbell for her.

This joint must cost him a fortune, she thought.

Chris opened the door and handed the bellboy a couple of bills as a tip. She apologized for being late as she walked inside.

"That's okay," he said. "Want a beer?"

"Only if it's Sam Adams."

"Is there any other kind?" He grinned and made his way to the kitchen. "Well, you look happy today. That must mean one thing. You heard from your friends."

"Yeah, and what a relief." Ellen went to the windows to take in the view. The windows ran from floor to ceiling and had automatic venetian blinds. She played with the switch, opening and closing them. "Turns out the message was a hoax, and nothing out of the ordinary is happening there. They'll be coming home soon."

"That's great." Chris handed her the beer, but with a sad look on his face. "Does that mean you'll be going home, too?"

Ellen's mood dropped. "Well, I have to go back to med school. I haven't even finished my first year."

Chris moved away from the window. "I figured you'd be leaving."

Ellen didn't look at him, afraid her eyes would get teary if she did. *I finally get a chance for a relationship with a decent guy, and I'm the one calling it off.* "Heck, New York and Boston are so close, we're practically neighbors."

Chris seemed to take her cue. "And there are dozens of commuter flights every day."

"If you could still afford to fly," Ellen said. "This place must cost a fortune. Why didn't you move into the corporate condos? It would have been much cheaper."

"I know, but those condos are so close to work. I'd be called in at all hours. Besides, your father keeps me so busy, this space gives me a place to decompress."

"Oh go ahead, blame it on Daddy. But I must admit, the view here is great." The suite overlooked Boston's harbor. It had scenic views of the piers, boats of every size, and fancy restaurants. A block away, Ellen even saw a large white tent with dozens of workmen outside. "What's that?" she asked.

Chris walked back to the window and looked down the street. "Oh, that's the Pavilion, an outdoor amphitheater. And you're right, it is big. It's supposed to seat five thousand people."

"In that tent? Wow. What are they getting ready for?"

"Beats me," he said, moving away.

The tent fascinated her, however. Workmen were constructing a huge cross at the entrance. Television and satellite trucks were all over the place. Workers laid cables and hung huge lighting grids. She squinted her eyes and was able to read the marquee at the entrance: *The Annual Easter Sunrise Worship Service, sponsored by the American Council of Conservative Christians.*

She cringed. "Remind me not to be around here on Sunday. The thought of five thousand right-wing Christians roaming the streets scares me to death."

"You've got that right," Chris said, taking a plastic bag out of his pocket. He held it out to her. "So, you want to catch a buzz?"

"You mean smoke a joint?" He nodded, and she nodded back. They made their way to the living room, but didn't sit on the couch. They moved the coffee table to the side and sat cross-legged on the rug.

Chris laid a couple of joints on the floor. He lit one and took a toke. He handed it to Ellen. She hadn't smoked pot on a regular basis for a while. In fact, she hadn't since graduating from Stratburgh. She and Chris took turns, but nothing happened until about her fourth toke. A sense of calm enveloped her. She even felt kind of floaty.

After a few more inhalations, she started getting high. It felt good, exciting and sexy. She wondered if Chris thought she was sexy. She offered him the roach. He inhaled deeply and moved toward her. As he got closer, she opened her mouth to accept his kiss. Their lips touched and he gently exhaled into her mouth. It was the most intimate moment she'd ever experienced. She loved him.

Chris took Ellen by the hands and led her to the bedroom. Panic surged through her, though. She'd never had to disclose her status under such intimate circumstances before. She feared he would reject her, especially since she'd waited until this moment to tell him. But she never expected this to happen so early in their relationship.

She stopped at the bedroom door. "Chris, I need to tell you

something." He looked into her eyes, and she wanted to cry. She bit her bottom lip. "I'm HIV positive."

"Oh," he said. Ellen's heart stopped. He smiled and gently touched her cheek with his fingers. "That's okay. We'll be safe."

He finished leading her into the bedroom and she closed her eyes. *I may have won at love after all.*

CHAPTER THIRTY-SIX

Good Friday

Zacchaeus tossed and turned on his mat. He threw his pillow to the side and put his hands under his arms to stop them from shaking. He felt like he had back at the Second Birth Treatment Center—like a nobody, without anyone caring if he lived or died. He figured Eddie was just saying those things to make him feel better. Obviously, Eddie didn't care for him and never had.

It was also obvious Sharar didn't have any affection for him, either. *A pissant faggot.* Zacchaeus knew he was missing essential qualities the rest of the Disciples had, yet he was anything but pissant. He was strong. He was certainly better-looking than Raamiah. Zacchaeus had thought that he and Sharar were developing a friendship, becoming confidants. He was Sharar's little soldier. Perhaps with time, he would even become his lover.

Or maybe I'm just being foolish again. I'm just a little man trying to be noticed in a world of important men. I'm truly forsaken.

The loudspeakers crackled and Mordecai called everyone into chapel. Zacchaeus looked out the window. It wasn't even dawn yet, hours before the service was scheduled to begin. Yet

Mordecai decided their day was to begin early on Good Friday, when the Faithfuls should be meditating about the Lord's ultimate sacrifice.

Zacchaeus got dressed to join the others in worship.

CHAPTER THIRTY-SEVEN

Mordecai stood next to the altar, looking officious. He liked that pose. It got attention, although he feared it made him look a little pompous, but his followers didn't seem to care.

He cleared his throat and began. "Faggots tell us that 'it gets better.' But I'm here to tell you that they're lying. Life may get easier for those faggots as the world kowtows to their propaganda. Their so-called fight for equality. And while life is getting easier for the sinners, it's becoming harder for the righteous, people like you and me."

He leaned in with a conspiratorial stance. "I have it on good authority that the two queers in our cellar even got married."

"No!" someone from the congregation cried.

"Oh, yes! The state of New York, in the ultimate concession to evil, allowed them the rites of holy matrimony. The state said their relationship was legitimate. But where does that put the relationships God sanctioned? The relationship you have with your wife or husband? With your children and grandchildren?"

Grandpa Swanson rose from his pew. "But I loved my wife, Edna. May she rest in peace."

"I know you loved Edna." Mordecai bowed his head for a moment, then jerked it back up. "But the gays are making fun of that relationship. Of your love, Grandpa. They're making fun of all of our loves. As if the years we've spent with our wives and husbands don't matter."

"But my love for Edna did matter."

"Of course it did. That's why we're going to turn the tables on sin, at least for those two homosexuals in the cellar. They're going to pay for their blaspheming. For them, it's going to get worse. I promise you, a lot worse."

The Faithfuls murmured thanks in their pews and Mordecai felt triumphant. He played the right chords in his sermon. Nothing got people riled up more than threatening their place in society.

Mordecai made sure to look at each individual with sympathetic eyes. It would draw them into his plans. "We tried to pray those two gays away, but it didn't work. Then we politely asked them to leave. The two sodomites still refused to go. It is now time to act. To raise the Brethren's staff and to strike down the abominations who inflict our lives with sin. Who erode our morals and threaten our way of life."

The congregation rose, their eyes filled with fear and contempt. "Faggots prey on our children," a mother cried.

"They spread AIDS," screamed another.

"They're sick and vile!"

Mordecai raised his hands. "You're right, dear Faithfuls. We can't let the world be subverted by immoral homosexuals any longer."

"I want to crack open faggot skulls," Grandpa screamed.

"And that's what we're going to do. In time."

"I want to kill the two faggots now."

"Grandpa, if we kill them now, others will only take their place. We must stop this scourge at its source and let the sinful world know that the Brethren stands for righteousness."

The congregation stood up and cheered. Mordecai's face almost revealed a grin.

"We have a new, important mission. Are you ready to take up that challenge?"

The congregation's cheers became ecstatic.

"Good. Saul has made a list of duties. As you leave chapel, be sure to check in with him. He'll let you know if you are to fight sin at one of its sources or take on the equally important task of staying here and protecting the home front from evil."

The Faithfuls scrambled toward Saul.

"We're finally working toward something worthwhile!" one person yelled.

Another answered, "Yes! We're protecting our way of life!"

They all raised their arms to heaven. "Mordecai is great. Mordecai is good. Mordecai will redeem me of my sins."

CHAPTER THIRTY-EIGHT

Ellen opened her eyes. The sun spread beams of light throughout Chris's large bedroom, making it bright and airy. She was tempted to stay in bed a while longer, breathing Chris's scent. He had already left for work. It was Friday, after all. But he'd left a note on the bedside table, and when she read it, she felt complete.

> *Ellen, meeting with your father's new security team tonight, so I'm not sure when I'll be home. Please feel free to kick back and relax. Affectionately, Chris*

The note was clearly an invitation for her to stay in his life, at least for one more day. Her hopes for a relationship were coming true, yet a twinge of regret still ran through her. Chris didn't sign the note *with love* or any other expression of intense feeling. *Affectionately* was how he might sign a letter to his grandmother. She knew it was silly. It was too early for a man to declare his love to another person, yet she wanted him to.

She decided to take Chris up on his offer and went into the kitchen to make coffee. A thermal carafe filled with Colombian dark roast waited for her, and she grinned at Chris's thoughtfulness. She poured a cup and went to the window to watch the workmen's progress with the Pavilion.

Only three more days until Easter morning, and Jamie's adventure was over before it started. She felt sorry for him. He wanted to be a hero again. To have a hero, there has to be a villain and victims. She decided not to think about Jamie's misfortunes and instead got out Chris's laptop to surf the web. She couldn't get online, though. She kept getting an error message asking her to provide a valid security authorization. She didn't have that thingamajig, the dongle. She thought of searching for an unsecured Wi-Fi hotspot, but it wasn't worth the hassle. She decided to take a shower instead.

Once she was clean, Ellen went into the bedroom to change. But the only clothes she had were the ones she'd worn last night, and the thought of greeting Chris in dirty clothes disgusted her. She opted to search his closet.

On the closet floor were a suitcase and several cardboard boxes filled with books. Even though it was snooping, she couldn't resist sneaking a peak at Chris's makeshift library. There were only a couple of classics, *The Great Gatsby* and *Elmer Gantry*. The rest were nonfiction. There were self-help books about clawing your way to the top of business world, investment strategies, and even some travel books for the Cayman Islands, Switzerland, and Belize. One book stood out as different, however—a textbook titled *Theologies of America's Religious Fringe.*

She picked up the heavy volume and papers fell from the inside cover. The first piece of paper was a weird listing of numbers—ten digits each, with spaces throughout each number. She had no idea what the numbers meant. But there were other interesting documents, deposit receipts from banks around the world. Most were for small amounts—a couple hundred bucks here, five hundred there. But there were some for higher amounts. She added up the receipts and they totaled almost $400,000.

She looked at the receipts again. They didn't have the account owner's name on them, only an account number. *But why would he have them if they weren't his? And who would be giving him so much money? Is he selling something? What could he sell, and who would be the buyers?*

She hoped the payments weren't for something illegal. With her smartphone she took pictures of each receipt before carefully returning them to the closet. Then she dialed her father's number. Marianne answered. "Can you have my father call me? I need to know about the employment research he did for Chris."

"Christian Donahue?" Marianne asked. She sounded surprised.

"Yeah. And I need to know the answer as quickly as possible."

CHAPTER THIRTY-NINE

Zacchaeus watched Saul divide the congregants into two groups. The strong and good-looking would travel with Mordecai to fight evil's onslaught. The sickly and the weak were to stay at the home front to defend the Brethren.

He wasn't sure if he should get a job assignment from Saul or not. Before last night, he was with the Disciples. Now he wasn't so sure he belonged with them. Sharar approached and put an arm around his shoulder in a manly embrace. "Are you excited, my little soldier?"

Zacchaeus didn't know how to respond. Did Sharar change his feelings? Was he no longer a pissant faggot? Or was he Sharar's soldier once again? Either way, he felt good having Sharar pay attention to him.

"Yes, Disciple. I'm very excited."

"Good, because we need to get started." Sharar left the chapel, and Zacchaeus quickly followed.

CHAPTER FORTY

Ellen sat in Chris's living room, biting her nails down to the quick. Her father hadn't called back and she considered contacting his private investigator to track down the information, but he wouldn't do anything without her father's permission. *No,* she thought. *I have to wait and talk with Daddy. If Chris stole money or corporate information from Rhodes Petroleum, he'd want to be the first to know about it.*

Her cell phone rang just as her cuticles started bleeding. Her father was on the other end. "What's so damned important?" he blurted out.

"I have questions about Christian."

There was a heavy sigh. "Will this take long? I have to get back to my meeting."

"I don't know, Daddy, but this is important. When you did your employment investigation on Chris, what did you find out?"

"We don't investigate our recruits. We vet them, there's a difference." He sounded indignant.

"Stop bullshitting and tell me what you found out."

He gave a guttural cough. "He came up clean as a whistle."

"Thank you." The answer gave her a calming sense of relief. But there was a tense pause at her father's end. "Daddy, is there anything more you should tell me?"

"In fact, his record came up unusually clean. Not even a parking ticket."

"What does that mean?"

"Well, unusually stellar background checks could indicate several possibilities. But the most probable explanation is that the person's real background isn't as faultless as they'd like people to believe."

"And you still hired him?"

He laughed. "Oftentimes, a shady background can be invaluable."

"And the possibility that he might be dishonest didn't concern you?"

"I'm neither his mother nor his minister, Ellen. As long as he gets his job done and doesn't steal from me in the process, I don't care."

His statement surprised her. "Daddy, what is Chris's job, anyway?"

"It's to do whatever I tell him to do."

"Including illegal things?"

"I would never tell an employee to do anything illegal. But many of my employees operate under a certain amount of autonomy. Do you understand what I'm saying?"

She did, and it disturbed her. "Daddy, I found some interesting paperwork in Chris's apartment today." She pressed on, telling him about the receipts and her fear Chris might be embezzling, or worse. "Daddy, wouldn't it be prudent to check these receipts out?"

"Probably," he answered. "But it would be a lost cause. No offshore bank will reveal the identities of their clients. I suppose we could pay someone to dig the information up, but it wouldn't be worth the expense."

"How can you be sure Chris isn't embezzling or trading proprietary information?"

"Chris may be doing that sort of thing," he said. "But I'm confident I'm not the victim. He doesn't have access to any of my financial accounts or any real proprietary information. His title is Corporate Liaison, but he's really just a contract spy."

"A contract spy? What is that?"

"You've heard of good cop/bad cop, haven't you? Same principle, only regarding contract negotiations."

Now she was completely confused.

"Look, during a negotiation with another company, Christian's job is to befriend the other side and gain their confidence. The information he gathers gives us an upper hand because we'll know the other side is thinking. But he's only worked one contract so far. And we weren't expecting much benefit out of that deal."

"What was it for?"

"It was for underwriting events for a large religious organization. We gave them a small gift, about fifty thousand dollars. In return, they'll mention Rhodes Petroleum positively in their sermons, and I'll even show up at a couple of their services."

"Thank you, Daddy."

"Then have I answered all of your questions? Because I have to get going."

"No, I have one more..." But Ellen was too late. There was a click on the other end, so Ellen swiped her phone off, too. She'd have to investigate Chris by herself. She got out her tablet and went to the window to prepare a to-do list. She couldn't think clearly, though. The workmen at the Pavilion kept diverting her thoughts. They were going full-tilt, setting up thousands of chairs and tripping over the television cables that were set up earlier.

At the tent's entrance, a larger sign replaced the first one. *Welcome to the National Easter Sunrise Service, presented by the American Council of Conservative Christians with generous support from the Rhodes Petroleum Foundation.*

She laughed. *Daddy's charity was in front of me the entire time. But why didn't Chris tell me anything about the service or Daddy's connection with it? What could be so important about an*

Easter service, even with live television coverage? She wondered if an answer could be found in his laptop, but she'd need his computer dongle to access the network.

Or maybe not.

She ran to Chris's closet and dug out the paper with the strange numbers. Using an unsecured Wi-Fi hotspot, she got online. The first thing she noticed was his browser was set to anonymous mode, meaning his browsing history and cookies would be deleted at the end of each session so there would be no record of the sites he visited.

She typed in the first set of numbers, the series of ten digits, separated with spaces. She replaced the spaces with periods and, sure enough, the numbers were IP addresses for web pages. The first page was a web anonymizer, a service that allowed the computer to surf the Internet anonymously. She typed in the next series of numbers. It opened a file hosting service on the Internet. She looked down the paper's row of numbers and typed the next one in. Sure enough, it was a password. Once inside the service, she saw a list of files that Chris had saved. They were a series of video clips from television news stations: Seattle, Minneapolis, and Los Angeles. She opened the first clip.

The anchor read from the teleprompter, "This morning, a gunman burst into the worship services of the Independent Fundamentalist Church of Minneapolis and started a shooting rampage." The broadcast cut to footage taken by a parishioner with his cell phone. The anchor continued, "The gunman's only victim was Reverend William Ashley, the church's associate pastor. No other casualties have been reported. But at this time, the police have no leads about the gunman or a possible motive."

The other clips were similar to the first. All shootings at a conservative church, and each time the gunman killed only one minister. No one else was hurt. As the congregants ran outside in terror, the gunman disappeared without leaving any clues.

She looked at the paper for more addresses. She recognized the next one and her heart missed a beat. It was the address that brought up the document that had wreaked havoc with her laptop.

The link between the Brethren and Boston is the National Easter Sunrise Service. The Brethren are planning to kill another pastor at the service!

She typed in the last address on the paper and found a dozen scanned receipts for rooms and banquet halls in this very hotel for Easter. It confirmed her fears. *I have to call the police. But what I'm about to tell them won't make sense. Why would the Brethren want to hurt a consortium of conservative churches? Weren't they allies in the fight against the liberals?*

She dialed 911. She realized she probably sounded like a ranting lunatic to them, and they were being polite. They took down her telephone statement and asked her to come by the station to be interviewed. She swiped the phone off, wondering if going down there would do any good. Deciding it was worth a chance, she turned around to get dressed. Chris was behind her.

He drew back his arm and delivered a wicked right hook.

CHAPTER FORTY-ONE

Sharar stood before the Disciples and meticulously outlined the strategies for Ground Zero. He finished with "It's late. We have very little time left, and a six-hour ride ahead of us. Since there's much to do when we arrive, we can't hesitate."

The Disciples took the hint, and so did Zacchaeus. He was part of the Disciples again, and he dove into his duties. His first chore was to prepare food for the trip. Easy-to-eat meals, high in protein and carbohydrates, for lasting energy. He also had to make sure the costumes were cleaned, pressed, and neatly packed.

When Zacchaeus finished, Sharar instructed him to do the real work. The *important* work. He was to pack the artillery and ammunition into five SUVs for their trip. The Disciples would be split up between four of the vehicles. The fifth was exclusively for the use of Sharar and his manservant—him, though he was almost a Disciple. One of the chosen.

Sharar gave him a knowing nod, then left to oversee the other Disciples.

Zacchaeus watched Sharar from afar. He couldn't help it. He loved the way Sharar looked—manly and strong, yet kind and compassionate. Sharar walked with confidence past the Disciples and divvied out words of encouragement and warning. "Step lively," he said. "Faster, Raamiah. Don't let that belly fat get in the way of destiny!"

Sharar looked over and saw Zacchaeus staring. In a loud

voice he said, "You're doing good, my little soldier. I'm proud of you."

Sharar continued with his duties while Zacchaeus basked in the compliment. But he began to worry when he saw Raamiah approaching Sharar. Raamiah's smile exposed his filthy brown teeth. Raamiah said something to Sharar, and Sharar got angry. They argued, and Sharar hit Raamiah. Raamiah fell to the ground and then looked up with hate in his eyes.

This made Zacchaeus happy, but what followed made his stomach turn. Sharar helped Raamiah stand up, and they embraced one another. Sharar even kissed Raamiah on the forehead.

Zacchaeus wondered how Sharar could show affection toward that man. He was fat, ugly, and mean. He didn't have spiritual thoughts. He loved evil. He loved dominating and striking fear into the hearts of Godly men.

Zacchaeus paused. *Could Sharar be like Raamiah? Maybe Sharar isn't as kindly as I believed. And maybe Sharar is using me for his own gain, so that I'll follow him without question.*

No, that's not possible. Sharar cares for me. He told me so himself. I'm his little soldier.

The two thoughts ricocheted back and forth through Zacchaeus's brain, and he started shaking.

Breathing slowly to control his tremors, he finished packing the SUVs. When no one was looking, he made his way to the Disciples' quarters to gather more supplies. He wrapped them in a linen cloth and hid them under his clothes, for fear someone would spot him carrying a bundle through the square.

He walked quickly past the Faithfuls guarding the home front. However, they didn't appear to be very weak. They were yelling the most obscene things about Eddie and Jamie. They had fierceness in their eyes. It frightened Zacchaeus, so he didn't speak to anybody.

He reached his destination, the Spiritual Containment Center, and closed his eyes, lowered his head, and prayed, "May the Lord have mercy on my soul."

He opened his eyes and walked to the guards. "Open the door and stand back," he commanded.

"But we can't. We're under strict orders from Saul. We're not even allowed to talk with the prisoners, and you want to go in there?"

"I'm under strict orders, too," he lied. He hoped his shaking hands didn't give him away. "And my orders come from Sharar. He has higher rank than Saul."

The guards conferred with each other. "Very well, then. But let it be known we comply under protest."

"Duly noted," Zacchaeus said.

The guards handed him a lantern and opened the cellar door reluctantly.

He thanked the guards with "God will bless you for your kindness."

"May Mordecai bless you, too," they said. He gave them an expression of gratitude and went through the door. The cellar was pitch-black, and smelled, too.

Jamie's voice came through the darkness. "Who is it?"

"It's me, Zacchaeus," he called back loudly, making his voice sound deep and manly. He didn't want to tip off the guards to what he was really doing. He held up the lantern to illuminate the room, and he heard Eddie gasp.

"We have nothing to say to Zacchaeus," Jamie said. "We will only speak with Andrew Caldwell."

Zacchaeus looked over at Eddie. "Is that true for you, too?"

Eddie slowly replied, "Yes. I'll only speak to my good friend Andy."

"So be it." Zacchaeus put down the lantern and his shoulders slumped. He retrieved the package from his pocket. "These are for you, from your old friend."

Jamie accepted the gift, untied the hemp string, and pulled back the linen fabric to reveal a handgun and a wad of cash.

"What is this?" Jamie asked.

Zacchaeus swallowed hard. "It's my undoing." He looked over at Eddie, who was crying.

Jamie asked, "What are we supposed to do with this?"

Zacchaeus's voice dropped to a whisper. "Wait until sundown. By then, the Disciples and the Faithfuls will have left. Security will be at its lowest. It should be easy for you to escape."

Jamie nodded. "Why is Mordecai doing all of this?"

"Mordecai is creating a diversion, something sinful his Faithfuls can latch on to."

"A diversion? What is he trying to cover up?"

"What he's going to do to his real enemies."

"Okay." Jamie paused to process Andy's garbled information. "First, who are Mordecai's real enemies? Where are they located? And what can we do to stop Mordecai?"

Zacchaeus shook his head. "You do what God required, but you don't have much time. It all begins on Easter morning."

He started to walk out, but Jamie stopped him again. "You're not making sense. Tell me, what begins on Easter morning?"

He turned around. "Armageddon begins."

"Armageddon against the gay community?"

"No," Zacchaeus said. "Mordecai's real enemies are the ones closer to his heart."

Jamie scrunched up his face, and finally said, "Okay. At least tell us where this Armageddon is going to start."

"Boston." Zacchaeus left the cellar. Fearing he'd been gone too long and his absence had been noticed, he hurried back to the Disciples' quarters.

CHAPTER FORTY-TWO

Mordecai watched one of the Faithful lead the stallion into the square. "Careful," he cried. "This magnificent animal is a symbol of our ministry." He approached the horse and petted its white mane. "My beautiful animal," he whispered into its ear. "Our time is nearing, just as the Archangel Ezekiel promised. And I'll carry my sword and wear my crown as I ride you to victory."

Mordecai signaled the worker to continue loading the horse, and he turned his attention to the Faithfuls preparing to leave for Boston. With the faggots as a common enemy, his flock were excited and ready. As a reward, he gave them signs of appreciation. Smiles. Handshakes. Even hugs. The sacrifice paid off. Victory was in his reach.

But I've got to act humble, he reminded himself. *I will be making a miraculous appearance as the leader of a ragtag group of humble righteous, showing mankind the way to heaven.*

His entrance into the city would have to be stealthy, because no one would recognize his divinity. But after D-Day things would be different. The Christian world would be in disarray, and he would step in to preserve order. Everyone would praise him for his selfless actions, and they'd come to worship him as the true voice of modern Christianity.

Mordecai got into in the lead SUV and Saul took the driver's seat. They drove down the path leading out of the compound, the vehicles filled with his hand-chosen Faithfuls following close behind.

Smiling at the size of the procession, he asked, "How many are coming with us?"

"About two hundred," Saul said.

"That should be plenty."

Saul drove up to the electronic gate and pressed the wireless remote. The gate rolled open, and Mordecai got on the SUV's loudspeaker. "Now is our time, Christian soldiers. We are marching with humility and reverence into Satan's lair. May the Lord's divine countenance be upon us."

The Brethren cheered and followed Mordecai out of the compound.

CHAPTER FORTY-THREE

Zacchaeus ran into the Disciples' area just as Sharar yelled, "Where's my manservant?"

"Here I am, Disciple." He tried to hide the shortness in his breath.

If Sharar noticed anything amiss, he didn't show it. "It's about time, Zacchaeus. You can't separate from the group once we're at Ground Zero. You've got to stay close by."

Zacchaeus understood and bowed with supplication. "Absolutely."

Sharar turned to the Disciples. "Mordecai will be taking the state and county roads with the Brethren because they have so many vehicles. It'll be easier for them to separate on those roads and not look conspicuous."

Raamiah stopped picking his teeth for a moment and asked, "What route will we use?"

"We'll take the expressways. That'll save up to an hour overall. But remember, from now on, we are to remain separate from Mordecai and the Brethren."

"That doesn't bother me in the slightest." Raamiah threw his toothpick on the ground and looked Sharar straight in the eye. "What I want to know is when do we get paid?"

Sharar sneered. "When your work is satisfactorily finished. Not a second before."

"Just asking, is all. Need to make sure my portfolio is properly diversified, you know." Raamiah laughed. The rest of the Disciples chuckled along, too.

Zacchaeus realized the Disciples weren't really disciples at all. They just wanted the money. They wanted to be paid in full.

The Disciples loaded into their SUVs and headed for the gate.

CHAPTER FORTY-FOUR

Early morning, Holy Saturday

The light snuck between the cracks of the cellar door, providing just enough illumination to show how filthy the dungeon was. Jamie and Eddie had been locked up there for hours, but Eddie hadn't said a word the whole time. He was probably blaming himself for Andy's troubles.

Andy's a fucked-up individual, Jamie thought. *But right now we've got our own problems.*

He turned to Eddie, but was only able to see his outline in the dim light. "Do you think it's time to escape yet?"

"No," Eddie answered flatly. "Andy told us to wait until sundown, and we're going to obey his wishes."

"Then how are we supposed to know when the sun sets? They took our watches, and there aren't any windows in this fucking cell. It could have set hours ago for all we know." Jamie started doodling again.

But Eddie evidently wanted to get something off his mind. "You know, Jamie, if we ever get back to New York…"

"You mean *when* we get back."

"Okay. *When* we get back to New York, I won't have a job anymore."

Jamie realized Eddie was worried about his own situation. "Don't be silly. Of course you'll have a job."

"No, Bardot was serious when he said I had to return for Easter brunch or else."

"He's not going to fire you for missing one day of work."

"Yes, he will, without a second thought."

Jamie wanted to swear again, but deep down, he knew Eddie was right. "I'm sorry," he said.

Eddie didn't answer. Or maybe Jamie couldn't hear his response because of the loud ruckus that started outside. It sounded like the Faithfuls had stormed the front of the cellar. They banged on the exterior walls, yelling the most disturbing things.

"Okay, maybe Andy's right," he said. "We should wait for things to settle down before trying to escape."

Eddie agreed, and Jamie stared at the wall until he fell into an uncomfortable sleep. What seemed like moments later, he awoke to an eerie silence. The Faithfuls' commotion had stopped. "Must be time to escape."

Eddie agreed and they put their plan into motion. Eddie quietly crawled to the front of the dungeon door and curled into a fetal position. Jamie grasped a plank of wood and hid in the background. He gave Eddie the signal to start wailing, which he did, pretty convincingly. Jamie figured it was due to all the pain and anguish pent up inside him. He finally had an opportunity to open his emotional spigot, and the pain just flowed out.

"What's wrong?" the guard asked from outside.

Eddie didn't stop wailing.

Jamie shouted, "He's in lots of pain. Saul took away the medicine for his leg, and the welts he got from Mordecai's whipping must have become infected. He needs help."

The guard said, "Just a moment."

Jamie heard the jingling of keys as the guard opened the door and stuck his head inside. Jamie sprang from his hiding place and walloped the guard's head with the piece of wood. He fell to the ground. He struck the guard again before he and Eddie walked outside. After making sure the coast was clear, they locked the guard inside.

The rest of the Faithfuls had moved into the square, gathering tree branches, logs, and kindling. It looked like they were in the process of making a big bonfire. There were a couple of crosses in the middle of the pile.

Eddie froze at the sight. "What do you think they're building that for?"

"They're building it for us." But Jamie noticed the Faithfuls' profane mutterings weren't just about them. They were also swearing about foreigners, non-Christians, and just about anybody who was different from them.

"How will we slip past the Faithfuls without being seen?" Eddie asked.

"We can't," he answered. "So our only hope is to blend in with them. If we act as crazy as they do, maybe they won't notice who we are."

Eddie gave him an *are-you-crazy* look. "How do you blend in with a bunch of maniacs?"

Jamie shrugged. He hunched his torso forward, keeping his head looking to the heavens. Then he jerked his arms in upward random swings and yelled, "Rush Limbaugh is God's voice on earth" and "The only good gay is a dead gay."

Jamie realized it didn't matter what he yelled. What mattered was that he looked like the rest of the Brethren, half-crazed.

Eddie surprised him. He play-acted insane with abandon.

Together, they walked in the direction of the parked SUVs. Jamie continued spouting conspiratorial theories while Eddie jabbered on in Spanglish. When they reached the galvanized steel fence encasing the motor pool, Jamie crossed his fingers. He hoped there would be at least one vehicle with the keys still in the ignition. But his luck ran out when they tried to open the gate. It was locked up tight with another one of those electronic locks requiring a code to open it.

"Not only that," Eddie said. "The combination has to be punched in with a certain rhythm. It reads the pauses as part of the code."

Jamie looked at him with disbelief. "How do you know that?"

"It says so right on the keypad."

Jamie looked closer. The keypad read, *Patent Pending: code and timing-spatial compliant security system.*

"Damn it," Jamie muttered. "Well, we can't stay here," Jamie went on. "We need to find a secure place to hide while we figure out how to get out of here."

He and Eddie started searching for a hideaway. They didn't get far before they heard sounds coming from the side of the pathway.

It was more like a high-pitched, nasal whimper, and it sounded like Peter Sokolov.

CHAPTER FORTY-FIVE

Ellen woke with a nasty-tasting cloth in her mouth. Her entire body ached, and she smelled offensive, too.

She tried to get off the floor, but her legs were bound. The tape started at her ankles and ran up to her knees. Her wrists were also bound with tape. Chris had even taped the window curtains closed.

The door rattled and he entered. "Promise not to scream?" he asked when he reached her. She nodded and he pulled the rag out of her mouth. "How long have I been tied up?" Ellen's throat was rough and scratchy.

"About a day." He chuckled. "You know, if you had stayed in New York and minded your own business, none of this would be happening." He found another roll of packing tape and started to reinforce the binding on her wrists.

She tried to fight him, but it was useless. She asked, "Why would the Brethren want to harm Conservative Christians? It doesn't make any sense."

"Very little about the Brethren makes sense." He tore off another strip of tape and wrapped it around her wrists.

"What do the Brethren plan on doing at the service?" He dropped the roll of tape and looked into her eyes. "They're planning to do what they did at those other cities, aren't they?"

He didn't answer her.

"Tell me!"

He sat down next to her. "Look, Ellen, the Easter Service was in danger of losing its funding. The council approached your father about giving additional money. The Brethren found out about it and paid me to make sure Rhodes Petroleum gave them the grant. That's all I was supposed to be concerned about."

"Supposed to be? What more did you do?"

"Stop asking me questions."

She struggled to get upright. "You're just as evil as they are."

He backed away. "I'm not evil. I simply provided information to the concerned parties. Considering what I could have done, I'm practically innocent."

Ellen laughed. "That's fucked up."

"Is it? If your father hadn't given them the money, the service would never happen, and neither would D-Day."

"Is that what you're calling it? D-Day?"

"I don't call it that. They do." He grabbed the rag and crammed it in Ellen's mouth. Within minutes he was out the door.

Ellen took a deep breath. She was still tied up and gagged, but at least she was alive.

CHAPTER FORTY-SIX

Jamie and Eddie ran to Peter, but cringed when they saw him. He was a mess. Horseshit still covered his clothes, and his face had been ripped open by the nails in the booby trap. Dried blood crusted over an eyebrow.

"Didn't anyone help you?" Jamie asked.

Peter shook his head. "I'm low on the priority list, compared to Mordecai's new mission."

"I'm sorry," Jamie said. "I'd like to help you, but how can I be sure you're not going turn on us again?"

Peter looked up with his good eye. "I'm sorry for the things I've done. But you're right. You don't have any reason to trust me."

"That's true," Eddie said. "We should stay far away from you. But coming out to yourself is one of the hardest things imaginable. Jamie and I know because we've done it. So I think you deserve another chance."

"No." Peter shook his head. "You've been my only friends, but look how I treated you."

Jamie gently rubbed Peter's tense shoulder. "You did what you had to do. We understand and we're not angry. Well, we're not angry with you, at least."

"But I should have known better."

"Maybe. But Eddie believes in you. And since I believe in Eddie, I'm going to give you a second chance, too."

Peter mouthed, *Thank you*.

"You're welcome," Jamie said. "But right now, we need to get you medical help."

Peter shook his head again. "The nearest hospital is too far away."

"Then we'll take you to the stables and Eddie will treat you." Jamie looked over to his husband. "There's enough medicine in that vet cabinet, isn't there?"

"Probably, but the stables are out of bounds." Eddie pointed across the compound. The Faithfuls had infiltrated the barn. Several of them were carting away bales of hay, probably to use as kindling for the bonfire. A couple of the others were emptying all the animal medicines onto the ground.

"It looks like we're out of options," Jamie said. "We need to escape."

Eddie shook his head. "Yeah, we need to get out of here. Unfortunately, all the vehicles are locked up tighter than Fort Knox."

"That shouldn't be a problem," Peter said.

"Sorry to contradict you," Jamie countered, "but we don't have a key to the motor pool gate."

Peter still grinned. "A key would be useless, anyway. The Brethren uses electronic locks, and you have to punch in a PIN number."

"I know that," Jamie said, slightly aggravated.

"But the locks are run by a computer system, and computers are hackable. If we can get into their network server, we can get into the motor pool."

"Great. Now you're telling me we need a computer genius."

"I used to hack computer systems." Peter smiled.

"Okay."

"I'm not lying," Peter said.

"Then let's get going."

Peter rose and grabbed Jamie's hand.

"But where's their server?" Eddie asked.

"In Saul's office, of course."

"In Saul's office? He's just Mordecai's administrative assistant, a paper jockey."

"He's a lot more than that. And all the servers are in his office."

"Really?" Jamie thought for a moment. "Because if we're going to convince the police to stop Mordecai, we'll need a lot more than just getting into the motor pool."

Peter nodded. "When it came to money and contracts, Saul had his hands in everything."

"That's good to know," Jamie said. "So Saul's place is probably the second most secure building in the entire compound. Right after Mordecai's own office."

Eddie nodded. "And I'm sure Saul didn't leave the doors unlocked."

"Probably not," Peter said. "But I can figure out the password he used."

Jamie got suspicious again. "How could you do that? Did he trust you enough to give the passwords?"

Peter averted his gaze. "No, he didn't trust me. But I think I can remember the pattern he used."

"A pattern? Those locks are extremely sophisticated and require a lot more than a pattern of numbers. Those numbers have to be timed just right."

"I know," Peter said. "They need a rhythm. And that's nothing more than a pattern of tones. And how does someone ensure the rhythm is done correctly? He sang a melody."

"A song?"

"Yeah. Saul's code was a song."

"If you say so, let's try it." Jamie started walking, but Eddie stopped him.

"We still have a problem," Eddie said. "On our way out, we'll have to drive past all the Faithfuls."

"Shit, you're right. So we're still screwed."

"No, we aren't," Peter said. "We can barrel through them, like in the movies."

Jamie shook his head. "Yeah, but we're in a zombie movie. And those zombies won't move out of the way for a speeding truck. And we can't run them over."

"Well, then we have to scatter the zombies first."

"How are you going to do that? Scare them so they'll run away?"

"Yeah."

"Okay." Jamie folded his arms across his chest. "And how are you going to do that?"

"Just follow me."

CHAPTER FORTY-SEVEN

Their trip to Saul's office was still fraught with danger from the zombie Faithfuls. Every time they encountered one of their swarms, the three would hide in the shadows until the coast cleared. Then they would make a mad dash to the next building. They crept along, building by building and swarm after swarm, until they reached the office.

At the entrance, Peter looked at the keypad's worn buttons and nodded. "Yep. I remember the song. 'Oh, when the Saints come marching in, oh, when the Saints come marching in.'"

Jamie shook his head. "Saul would sing something that stupid. But I think it needs to be faster. He'd be in a hurry to get into his office, so he'd sing it faster."

Peter picked up the beat and punched in the access code. *1369 1369 13693132.* The bolt made an unhinging sound and the door opened.

Carefully walking inside, they were surprised to see their images plastered over a bank of six security monitors, each twenty-two inches high. The images quickly changed to a video shot inside the chapel. Then it continued to rotate through different locations around the compound.

"Shit," Eddie said. "Looks like security at Yankee Stadium."

Jamie was surprised, too. The cameras were so well hidden

he'd never spotted them around the compound. The other side of the office had rows of computers lining an entire wall.

Jamie wondered why he didn't get caught when he and Eddie had surveyed the area earlier. Was Mordecai waiting for a better reason to catch them? He didn't have time to figure it out. Peter sat down at the computer desk, rolled up his sleeves, and promptly said, "Shit."

Jamie ran to his side. "Is something wrong?"

"Yeah, something's wrong. I forgot about Saul's dongle."

"I don't know what that is," Jamie said. "But if we need it, we'll find it. What does it look like?"

"It sort of looks like a flash drive, and it slips inside a USB port."

Eddie interrupted. "If it's so important, wouldn't Saul have taken it with him?"

"It wouldn't do him any good, except here, for this specific computer."

"Okay," Jamie said, thinking. "Then he would store it nearby, and in a safe place, right?"

"No," Peter countered. "He'd keep it close at hand, like on a keychain."

"Or how about in his clipboard?" Jamie picked up Saul's portable office and opened the bottom compartment. Hidden beneath a bunch of miscellaneous paperwork, Jamie found a little plastic piece with a metal knob at the end. "Kind of small for such a big computer system, isn't it?"

"The size doesn't matter," Peter said, smiling. "It's what you do with it that counts." He inserted it into the port. The familiar startup chord played, and the computer demanded a password.

"Shit," Jamie said.

"Not this time." Peter smiled and shook his head. "I bet Saul used the same password over and over again, like most people do." He hummed the hymn again, and punched in the password. They waited in suspense as the monitors went from black to white to blue.

Jamie patted Peter on the shoulder. "You're a digital whiz, aren't you?"

"Kind of. Growing up, I spent lots of time on computer newsgroups, learning how to hack systems." Peter bent over the keyboard and typed in a command. Nothing happened. He typed it again. Still nothing happened.

"What's wrong?" Jamie asked.

"I can open the motor pool locks, no problem. But all the other documents you wanted are gone. Saul must have wiped his hard drive clean." Peter quickly typed in more commands, but the computer gave him the same response. "Saul erased all the other drives, too. Even the backups."

"Can you recover any of the information?"

"Maybe, but it would take a lot of time."

"Shit," Jamie said. "Time is something we don't have."

"You're right." Eddie pointed at the security monitor. The Faithfuls were ransacking the dormitory, and the chance to get past them was getting less likely. "We got to get out of here. Now."

Peter's face brightened. "Don't worry. I have a solution." He hunched over the keyboard, launched an Internet browser, and started surfing away.

"Saul didn't erase the web browser?" Jamie asked, incredulously.

Peter didn't take the time to look up. "He couldn't. A browser is an intricate part of every operating system. Even if you think you've uninstalled it, it's still there, lurking in the background."

"Then let's give him some room to work," Jamie told Eddie. They moved to the back of the room while Peter did his thing.

❖

After several hours of nonstop work, Peter announced, "I'm ready."

Jamie and Eddie scrambled to his side and hovered over

his shoulder. "Are you sure this will buy us enough time?" He shrugged his shoulders and punched the *play* button on his computer. Loudspeakers throughout the compound burst into a static-filled tone—the kind the Emergency Broadcast Service plays to get people's attention before announcing a public emergency.

Jamie looked over at the security monitor and saw the Faithfuls, like a herd of sheep, begin listening as an electronic voice replaced the static tone. "This Emergency Broadcast Service alert has been activated by the president of the United States. This is not a test, and normal programming has been suspended. Please stay tuned for further instructions."

"Oh, this is great!" Eddie said.

"It doesn't have to be great," Jamie added. "It just has to work." He looked down at Peter. "This is going to work, isn't it?"

"I don't know," Peter confessed. "But we'll find out soon enough."

It didn't take long for the Faithfuls to react. They began running around the compound, yelling and screaming.

Then the loudspeaker continued. There was a rattling sound of a microphone being moved.

"My fellow Americans, this is your president. We have encountered a disaster of biblical proportions. Thirty minutes ago, terrorists shut down our country's defenses and currently occupy the Atlantic and Pacific coastlines. In a matter of time, they will have overrun the entire nation. Our country's only chance of survival is with the American people. Please, if you love your country, gather supplies and armaments. Take shelter in the wooded wilderness and start a militia. It is our country's only chance for survival against the godless—"

The announcement came to a halting stop. The Faithfuls stopped running around, too. They scattered.

A loud alarm rang and the security monitor quickly shifted to a shot of the main gate. Jamie saw the Faithfuls approach the gate as if they were going to storm it. "Oh my God," Jamie yelled. "We've got to shut off the power to the gate."

Peter searched the network to find a program to control the gates, but he couldn't find anything. Jamie and Eddie watched the monitors, helpless.

As the first Faithfuls arrived at the gate, they grasped the chain links like they were going to climb the fence. Cracking sounds came over the audio, and a flash of flames accompanied by horrid-sounding screams. Most of the Faithfuls fell off, their hands burned. The ones with a strong grasp on the fence weren't as lucky. The skin on their palms fused with the fence's links. They finally fell, dead. Jamie could see pain and fright on their charred faces.

The electrical current took a toll on the fence, and the connections burst into flames. The lights around the gates flickered and burned out. The only thing Jamie could see on the monitors was the blurry mound of dead bodies. But that didn't stop the rest of the Faithfuls. They climbed over to escape to the other side. Others pushed at the burnt gate until it swung open, and the rest of the Faithfuls ran through.

Jamie opened the door and looked outside. The compound was abandoned. He shot a look back at Eddie and Peter. "Let's get out of here."

CHAPTER FORTY-EIGHT

Peter reached the door first, his hand on the keypad ready to go. But Jamie changed his mind. He took Peter's hand away and blocked the exit. "We can't leave. Not yet."

"Why?" Eddie asked, pointing to the security monitors. "The Faithfuls aren't a threat anymore. You saw that for yourself."

"I know, but we still need provisions." He turned to Peter. "Do you know where our cell phones are?"

Peter hunched his shoulders. "Yesterday Saul called his contacts and sold them on the black market."

"There's a black market for cell phones?"

"Yeah. Especially the new ones."

"Then we'll pick up a couple of throwaways on the drive to Boston." Jamie pulled out the handgun Andy had given him. "Next, we need more weapons. This is the only gun we have between the three of us. We need at least two more. With lots of ammo."

Eddie nodded, and Jamie asked again, "Peter, do you know where the guns and ammunition were stored?"

Again, he shrugged. "Saul used me to program his computers, not to fight."

"That's okay," Jamie said. He took the lead, running to the Disciples' quarters. Eddie and Peter followed. They were careful in case any Faithfuls were still roaming the compound. But the coast was clear, and they reached the Disciples' quarters. The Faithfuls had broken the windows and torn down the doors. Inside, it looked like the Faithfuls had fought terrorists. Cushions were ripped apart. Cupboard doors dangled on broken hinges. All the food had been taken, and streaks of blood ran down the walls. "Where would they have kept the weapons?" he asked. *The Faithfuls couldn't have taken them all. Where would the Disciples hide spare guns? Somewhere within easy reach in case they needed them in a hurry.* He scoured the rooms. He looked under the beds and pulled out the dresser drawers.

If the Disciples thought the authorities might infiltrate them, they would have built well-disguised places to hide their weapons, he realized. He started looking for trapdoors under the carpets and false backs on dressers. He noticed a closet in the main room. From the outside, it appeared to be very large. But when he opened the closet doors and looked inside, it seemed much smaller.

"I need a sledgehammer. Or a crowbar," he cried out. After a moment, Eddie returned with a couple of hammers. "Well, it's better than nothing," Jamie said, and started knocking down the plasterboard. Eddie joined him. They found a false wall concealing about a dozen handguns and rifles and several cases of ammunition.

They ran to the motor pool. Jamie was surprised the gate opened so easily, but the only vehicles left were a couple of rusted-out vans.

They picked out the biggest one, and Jamie asked Eddie, "Will you drive?"

Eddie nodded, and the three climbed inside. There wasn't much room—boxes filled the back of the van. "What are those?" Jamie asked.

Peter gave him a shrug and started taking out the boxes. "Looks like a bunch of medicines for farm animals."

Jamie practically jumped with happiness. "Let's go through them and see if there's something to treat Peter with."

"Yeah," said Eddie. "But let's do it after we're outside the compound. So, who has the keys?"

Jamie slumped over the dashboard. "Damn!"

From the backseat, Peter suggested, "Check the ashtray."

Eddie slid it open, and they were there. "How did you know where they'd be?" he asked.

"My father once took over a used car dealership. That's where they kept the keys."

Eddie started the truck and drove to the main gate. The charred remains of the Faithfuls disturbed Jamie. He looked over at Eddie, sitting behind the wheel, his head turned away from the carnage. In the backseat, Jamie saw Peter sitting quietly, yet quivering.

"Am I responsible for their deaths?" Jamie asked.

"No," Eddie replied. "Mordecai is responsible for all of this."

Jamie said, "We can't be disrespectful to the dead. Let's find another way over the fence."

Eddie turned the van to the left and followed the fence until he spotted a battered section. He backed up the van a good distance away from the section, put the vehicle into drive, and gunned the engine. It rammed into the fence, which crumpled to the ground.

As they neared the public road, Jamie asked him to pull over. "It's safe. Let's see if there's any medicine that can help Peter." He climbed into the back and read the names as he pulled out the little boxes. It sounded like he was speaking a foreign language. "Colvasone. Deccox. Ketamine hydrochloride."

"Was Mordecai becoming a drug dealer?" Eddie asked. "On the street they call ketamine Special K. It's popular at all-night dance parties."

"Well, we'll put that one away." Jamie took out another

bottle. "I think we've found the one we need. Vetericyn. Bovine Eye Wash."

"For cows?" Peter asked.

"Just lay back, Elsie. The label says the formula was cleared by the FDA to treat humans." Jamie gently placed Peter's head in his lap and flushed his eye with the solution. "How do you feel?"

Peter sat up and blinked a couple of time. "Better, I guess. Thanks."

"Great." He handed the bottle to Peter. "It also says you should apply it as often as necessary. Let's hope it works."

Eddie started the van and continued down the hill. When they got close to where they'd hidden the rental car, he looked over at Jamie.

"We can't stop," Jamie said. "We don't have the time. You know that."

"I do. But we have to make the time," Eddie said firmly. "When we get to Boston and go to the police, we'll need identification. Without it, the police will think we're homeless lunatics."

Jamie nodded. "But we can't take much time."

Peter spoke with a shaky voice. "You can't get your IDs, anyway."

"Why not?" Jamie asked.

"Because they aren't there." He looked down at his lap. "Saul told me that the park police found the car and Mordecai bribed the officer to give him everything you left in it."

"Then Mordecai has our wedding rings, too." Jamie closed his eyes.

Eddie patted his leg. "It'll be okay."

"I suppose." Jamie said as he wiped away a tear. "But what burns me is that Mordecai had his grubby fingers all over our rings. Even if we get them back, I'm not sure I'd be able to wear it without thinking of him."

"Then we'll buy new ones," Eddie said. "We bought those used on Craig'slist, after all."

"Step on it, we've got to get going." Jamie closed his eyes. He still had no idea who Mordecai's victims would be, or even what was going to happen. Only that it was something Armageddon-like.

CHAPTER FORTY-NINE

At a deserted section of highway, Eddie pulled over to look at the map. "Fuck," he said as he placed his finger at their location and followed the nearby roads.

Jamie watched, concerned. "What's wrong?"

"According to this map, we have to cross Lake Champlain by ferry."

"So?"

"This late at night, the ferry's going to be closed. To avoid the lake, we'll have to go farther south. It's going add a lot of time."

Jamie got worried. "How much time?"

"An hour. Maybe two."

"Can we take a northern route?"

"Yeah, we have two choices. We could go through Canada, but we don't have passports. And if we take U.S. Route 2, it would take forever."

"Then we drive south."

Eddie drove on in silence, while Jamie worried about what they would encounter in Boston. As they drove over a hill, Jamie spotted a speck of light in the distance. "Eddie, is that a gas station up there?"

Eddie squinted. "Maybe."

"Do we need gas?"

"No. Not really."

"Let's stop anyway. Hopefully, it'll have a store attached and we can buy some throwaway phones."

"Sounds like a plan."

❖

It didn't take long for the speck of light to grow into a sign for a gas station. They stopped, and Jamie ran inside. It was barely a gas station, and didn't sell anything but gas and oil. Not even a soda machine. A skinny teenager sat behind the counter, thumbing through a magazine featuring monster trucks. He wore headphones, and Jamie could hear the hard rock banging through the ear buds. He tried to yell above the music. "Can I use your cell phone, please?"

"Fuck you," the teen said, not looking up or even taking the headphones off.

"I'll pay you for the call."

The teen glanced at him. "How much?"

"Five bucks?"

"Not unless you give me two of them."

"Okay," he yelled, taking out a ten from the money Andy gave him. "The phone's not set to privacy or anything, is it?"

"Nah," the teen said. "Nothing's ever private around here." Jamie grinned and quickly punched in Ellen's number. It rang for about two minutes and finally went to voicemail.

Jamie covered his mouth and turned away from the teen because the music was so loud. "Ellen, it's me. That message in the package we got was right. Andy Caldwell sent it. Something's going to happen in Boston. A massacre, or something Armageddon-like. We're on our way and will be there in about five hours. We don't have our phones anymore. I had to borrow this one, so you can't even call me back. But I'll call you again as soon as I can. Love you, girlfriend." Jamie handed back the phone and ran back out to the SUV. "No luck," he said, slamming the door closed.

Eddie pulled out of the lot. "I saw you talking on a phone, though. Were you able to talk with Ellen, at least?"

"No. I left a message, but she can't call us back, obviously."

"Who's Ellen?" Peter asked from the back seat.

"She's our best friend." Jamie paused. "We've been through a lot together."

Over the next hour, Eddie stopped at every open gas station and convenience store. None of them carried cell phones. At a couple of places, Jamie was able to borrow a phone to call Ellen. But he never got through. Eventually, he gave up.

Then, twenty minutes farther down the highway, Eddie pointed to a large, well-lit sign. "In two miles, there's another gas station."

"Forget it," Jamie said, dismissing the idea with a flip of his hand. "We might as well wait until we're near Boston or some suburb." Eddie looked at him, and Jamie pulled out his wallet. "I have a little more than a hundred and fifty dollars left from the stash Andy gave us. If I continue to bribe the attendants, I won't have enough money to buy phones or the minutes to use them."

"Well, we might get lucky this time," Eddie said. "It's a Rhodes Petroleum gas station."

The Rhodes gas station looked more like a miniature Walmart than a gas station. Jamie figured it probably sold as much food and merchandise as gasoline. He went to the front counter, where three young women worked the cash registers. "Excuse me, do you sell any pre-paid phones and phone cards?"

"Sir, you've come to the right place," the first girl said. She sounded like she had her lines memorized. "At Rhodes Petroleum, we've got everything you need for the road. Follow me."

The attendant escorted Jamie down an aisle, as if they were

in an expensive department store. She presented a complete shelf of cell phones, accessories, and phone cards. All locked up behind a glass cabinet, of course. "What kind of telecommunication services do you need, sir?"

"I want three of the cheapest phones you've got. Plus plenty of minutes to go with them."

"But for a slightly larger investment, you can have a smartphone, with an actual keyboard."

"Don't need it. We're only making calls. What's the cheapest phone you've got?"

"Very well, then." She pointed at a refurbished Talk Till You Drop brand.

Jamie never heard of that brand before. "Will it have any service?"

"Of course, sir." She answered politely. "Talk Till You Drop purchases airtime from all the major cellular companies, so you'll never encounter a dead spot."

"Good," Jamie said. "I'll take three of them, plus charging cables for the van, and several hours of prepaid time." The attendant unlocked the cabinet and picked out the requested merchandise.

When they returned to the register, Jamie slapped money onto the counter and started ripping the phones from their hard plastic cases. "How do we activate these things?"

"Oh, that's easy," she said, ringing up the order. "You do it online."

Jamie looked up at the woman. "We're in a van. We don't have online access."

"That's okay." The woman reached underneath the counter and pulled out her purse. "You can use my personal smartphone."

"How much will that cost me?" he asked, reservedly.

"It won't cost you anything." The woman appeared shocked. "It's only a couple megs of downloading."

Jamie felt embarrassed. "Thank you, miss."

Back in the van, Jamie handed out the cell phones, and they plugged them into the cigarette lighter outlets. He hoped it wouldn't take long to charge them enough to use.

CHAPTER FIFTY

Ellen's fingers ached as she continued to scrape at the packing tape around her wrists. It felt like her nails had been ripped off her fingers, leaving only raw skin underneath. She touched the small, ragged hole she was making. It was maybe an eighth of an inch wide. She twisted her wrists in an effort to make the hole larger, but it didn't work. She needed another tactic.

If I could stand up, maybe I could find something to cut the tape with. But as much as she tried, she couldn't get off the floor with her arms tied behind her back. She took a deep breath and tried to maneuver them under her taped legs. She wasn't flexible enough.

Perhaps if I could sit on a chair, I could push myself up. She scooted toward the furniture. Holding her legs against the floor, she wiggled her back into the sofa. The strain made her upper legs sting, but she got on the cushions finally and started rocking back and forth. Reaching the proper momentum, she gave her body an added push. She was up, but tilting precariously. She held her breath and found her balance.

Spotting a coffee mug in the kitchenette, she hobbled her way there, penguin-like, and picked the cup up with her hands. Even though she couldn't see where she was aiming, she tossed the mug against the wall. It hit the refrigerator and broke into several pieces, which scattered on the tiled floor.

Slumping to the ground, she fumbled for a shard and picked one up, cutting her finger in the process. A smile appeared on her face. *I've got a perfect tool!* The more she scraped the tape with the broken earthenware, the larger the hole grew. Then, with a little pressure from her wrists, the tape broke.

Once she freed her legs, she knew what to do first: contact the police and convince them to stop the Brethren. But Chris had taken the phones, his computer, her backpack, and clothes. He'd taken his papers that would prove she was telling the truth. She tried to remember the IP addresses and passwords, but couldn't; she would have to try to convince them without proof. She ran to his closet and put on a pair of his jeans and a T-shirt. The clothes were so big on her she looked ridiculous, but it couldn't be helped.

She ran downstairs and asked the night desk clerk to let her use the phone. He just stood there, staring at her. She grabbed him by the collar and yelled, "I need to call the goddamn police."

He handed her the phone, but instead of calling the police, she called her father. She knew he'd want to be the first to be told about Christian. He didn't answer, though, so she left a message. "Daddy, it's me. Don't go to the National Easter Service. Deranged members of a cult named the Brethren are planning to storm the service and assassinate someone, most likely one of the pastors. Christian Donahue is part of the conspiracy. He kidnapped me to keep me silent. But I escaped and am going to the police station to file charges. Please call me back as soon as possible."

She hung up the phone, but decided against calling the police. She figured she'd be more persuasive in person. But before she could go there, she needed to change out of Christian's clothes and get her phone service working again.

As she drove to Dedham, she kept running through the facts as she knew them. They didn't add up. Why would the Brethren kill ministers from conservative churches around the country?

And why would they want to kill a pastor at the Easter Service in Boston? What would they gain?

She had the on-duty maintenance person open the doors to her condo once she arrived there. She changed clothes, grabbed her spare AmEx card, and took off for the nearest discount store, where she bought a prepaid cell phone. After a quick trip on the Internet, she was able to reprogram the settings for her phone's forwarding service and connect to her contact list. Now her new phone was as good as her old one.

Getting inside the Porsche, she gave Jamie another call. Still no answer, and her worries increased. *Obviously the text messages I got the other day were faked. Jamie and Eddie weren't singing "Kumbaya" by a campfire. For all I know, they could be dead.*

She arrived at the station house, but the officer at the desk didn't hear her come in. His head was buried in paperwork. "Excuse me, Officer. I need to make a report. I was kidnapped."

That got his attention. He looked up and pushed the bridge of his glasses against his nose. "Are you all right?"

"Yes. I'm fine. I was kidnapped by Christian Donahue because I found out about a plot he was involved with to assassinate a pastor at the National Easter Service that's going to take place at the harbor."

The officer's face remained emotionless. "Let me call an officer to take your report. Will you have a seat?" He got on the phone without taking his eyes off Ellen.

Moments later, the second policeman showed up and took her to a room where she blurted out everything she knew about Easter Sunday.

The officer wrote it all down. "That's a lot to take in, miss," he said as he put down his pen. "Do you have any copies of the documents you talked about?"

She shook her head.

"What about the letter you got on the papyrus paper?"

"I don't have that either."

"Do you have any proof to back up your claims?"

"No, but I remember the name of the hotel where the Brethren are staying in Boston."

"That's a start," the officer said. "But the first thing we'll do is put out a bulletin to find your Christian Donahue. We need to ask him some questions."

Ellen became concerned. "There's so little time left, sir. You need to stop the Easter Service before anything bad happens."

The officer nodded. "We'll certainly inform the American Council of Conservative Christians about this. We'll also ramp up our security for the event. But without proof, I'm afraid we can't force the council to cancel the event."

"Even though I was kidnapped to keep quiet?"

"That's one of the reasons why we're putting out the APB. We'll contact you as soon as we make any progress."

"Thank you," Ellen said, not certain there was anything to be thankful for. "Am I free to go?"

"Yes," the officer said. "But I suggest you visit a friend or a relative instead of going home."

"That's okay," she told them.

"Would you like us to add another patrol car to area around your condo, just to be safe?"

"That would fine." She left the precinct and realized the officer was right. If Chris discovered her missing, that's the first place he'd look for her.

As she left the precinct parking lot, her phone rang. She answered and Jamie shouted, "It's about time. Have I got things to tell you!"

She didn't give him a chance. She started unloading what she discovered. "The Brethren is planning to assassinate someone at the National Easter Service for the Council of Conservative Christians."

"The homophobic churches?" Jamie asked.

"Yeah. The Brethren plans on killing one of their pastors."

"Girlfriend, they're not going to assassinate just one pastor. They're going to kill everyone at that altar."

"Oh, my God." Her hands shook and her feet trembled. "Daddy's going to be up there with them. He'll be a victim, too."

CHAPTER FIFTY-ONE

Easter Sunday

Eddie pulled off the road and pulled out his map. Jamie looked over his shoulder, and they tried to find the location of the all-night diner where they were to meet Ellen.

"Well, here's Framingham." Eddie pointed to a little dot on the map. "So if the place is just down the road, it should be easy to find."

Jamie worried anyway. It was already Sunday—half past midnight. In six hours the Easter Service was scheduled to begin. Eddie drove on, and fifteen minutes later they pulled into the diner's parking lot. Jamie spotted Ellen's red Porsche. When they got inside, however, he hardly recognized Ellen. She looked tired, defeated. Her bruised fingers almost matched the color of her hair.

They sat opposite her in the booth. She pointed at Peter and asked, "Who's he?" She didn't even smile.

"My name's Peter Sokolov," he said, taking her finger and shaking it. "I'm Jamie and Eddie's friend."

Ellen looked over to Jamie for further explanation. "We met him at the Brethren. But it's okay. He's cool."

"Good to meet you, Peter." Ellen signaled the waitress. "I

already put in some food orders. They've been keeping them warm until you got here."

"Thanks," Jamie said. "But we don't have time to eat. We need to debrief. Ellen, you notified the police, right?" She nodded. "Good. What happened?"

"Basically, not much. I gave them a report. Well, as much as I could. They said they'd look into it."

"They're not stopping the service?"

"No. They said they couldn't because I didn't have any evidence to show them. It was only my word."

Jamie and Eddie didn't have any evidence, either. "Then what are the police planning to do? Sit on their butts while the apocalypse happens?"

"No, Jamie. The police notified the Council of Conservative Christians. It's up to the council to decide whether to cancel the service or not. But until they do, the police are increasing their security around the harbor area. They've already put out bulletins to apprehend Christian for questioning. And they're tracking down the Brethren to question them as well. If they see or hear anything suspicious, they'll act. But until then, they can't do anything."

Jamie took a breath and tried to settle down. "Well, thank goodness *we* can do something. Okay, what do we know about the service?"

Ellen explained how Chris had facilitated Rhodes Petroleum's involvement with the service. She also told them about the video clips she'd seen on his computer and about the creepy document that had messed up her laptop, and how it described Mordecai as the White Horseman of the Apocalypse.

"What's that, again?" Jamie looked over at Eddie.

"It's from the Book of Revelation," Eddie said. "'And there before me was a white horse! Its rider held a bow, he was given a crown, and he rode out as a conqueror bent on conquest.'"

"So that explains the dye we found in the stables." Jamie sat back in the booth. "Ellen knows as much as we do. Except we did find out who sent us the message."

Ellen leaned forward. Eddie started rubbing his eyes, and Jamie continued, "Andy Caldwell sent it to us."

"Andy?" Ellen exclaimed.

"Yeah. He joined the Brethren after leaving the Second Birth Treatment Center. But he's messed up. He's lost touch with reality."

Ellen turned to Eddie and took his hand. "I'm so sorry. I hope you're okay."

Eddie gave her a weak smile and nodded. Jamie was shocked. Was he the only person who didn't know how much Eddie cared for Andy? How could he have been so blind? He glanced over at his husband and took his hand. Taking a deep breath, Jamie looked back at Ellen and got back to business. "Everything makes sense. Let's see if we agree."

On the counter, Ellen made a mock-up of the harbor's pavilion area, using the salt and pepper shakers, the cups and silverware. "This is the Pavilion, where everything is going to happen," she said. "But unlike the earlier attacks on churches around the country, this won't have a lone gunman."

Jamie nodded. "No. They'll have multiple targets. The different leaders of the American Council of Conservative Christians."

Ellen stopped him. "There's one more victim, Jamie. My father."

"But you called him, right? Told him not to go."

"I tried. I left lots of messages, but he hasn't called me back."

Jamie took hold of her hand. "At least your father has his own security team."

Ellen nodded. Then she started shaking. "No, he doesn't. He's got a new security team, and it was chosen by Christian."

"Then we need to get to the harbor as quickly as possible."

When the four got outside, Jamie pulled Ellen aside. "You

know, the irony that a bunch of gays are saving a group of homophobic church leaders hasn't escaped me."

"It is kind of funny," Ellen replied.

Jamie gave her a sly smile in return. "Why don't you ride with us? It'll save time."

Ellen didn't need to answer. She got into the back of the van with Peter and came upon the big cardboard box. "What the hell is all this?"

"Veterinary medicine. It was in the van when we stole it from the Brethren's car pool." Jamie answered. "We've been treating Peter's eye with the eyewash we found."

Peter took the wash from the box and handed it to her. She checked the medical app on her phone and said, "It should be safe. Basically, it's just water and a tiny bit of mild bleach solution. Let me take a look at that eye."

Peter scooted toward Ellen as she wiped her hands with a wet-nap. She raised his eyelids with her fingers and took a look. "It appears that wash is doing a pretty good job," she said. "Even on a human."

Ellen threw the eyewash back into the box and looked at the other medicines. She held up the vials of ketamine. "Were they planning to knock someone out?"

Jamie gave her a blank stare. "Why? What's the stuff used for?"

"In hospitals, it's an anesthetic, essentially it 'cuts off' the brain from the body. But on the street it's sold as a date rape drug."

Eddie looked at them from behind the wheel. "Ellen, which way do I go?"

Ellen didn't have to think. "Head east, and follow the signs to Boston Harbor."

CHAPTER FIFTY-TWO

Mordecai knelt in a near-empty banquet hall. If he listened hard enough, he could hear his Faithfuls on the other side of the room's movable wall. They toiled for the glory of Christ. Mordecai dubbed their hall the Son-Shine Room. He named his the King of Kings. Mordecai's heavenly robes and crown tenderly rested on a table beside him.

He lifted his arms up to God and prayed. "My Father in heaven, I willingly accept the fate you have given me. I know that when my work is finished, you'll summon me to sit next to you and alongside my heavenly brother, Jesus."

Then it happened, just as it had happened before. Ezekiel, the archangel of transformation and death, appeared in front of him. The rays of golden sunlight emanating from the angel nearly blinded Mordecai. "Fear not," Ezekiel said. "For God has chosen you to change the world."

Ezekiel picked up the robe and draped it over Mordecai's shoulders. He put the golden crown on his head and held up the Lord's mighty sword for him to take. Mordecai grasped God's weapon, but he shook with apprehension and dropped it. Mordecai was tired, and his sweat fell like drops of blood.

"Do not worry," Ezekiel told him. "Our heavenly father knows your work is hard. The world refuses to recognize your divinity. In the beginning that was necessary, and the way God intended."

Mordecai nodded with understanding.

"But now your time has come. The world will recognize the false prophets that currently rule the earth. And as you take your place at God's side, mankind will bow before you."

Mordecai took Ezekiel's hand. In that moment, a knock came from the side door, and the Archangel Ezekiel returned to heaven.

"Who is it?" Mordecai asked angrily.

Saul opened the door. "Sorry to interrupt, but we have a situation out here."

"A situation?" Mordecai didn't like that word. It meant trouble.

"A couple of cops want to speak with you."

"Tell them I'm busy."

"That might not be wise."

Mordecai took a deep breath. "Very well." He took off his robe and crown and placed them back on the table.

As Mordecai entered the Son-Shine Room, he addressed the officers with a thunderous voice. "Who is it that seeks me?" They approached in their dress uniforms. They took off their eight-pointed hats and flashed him their identification and badges.

Mordecai stretched his neck, examined their IDs, and looked over to Saul. "Write down their badge numbers," he instructed. Saul obliged. "What do you want from me?" Mordecai asked.

The cop who appeared to be the leader casually walked around the room looking at everything. "Your appearance has raised some eyebrows around the harbor."

"There's nothing illegal about that, is there?"

"No, but the trailer with the white horse inside is parked illegally."

Mordecai shot a look at Saul, who snapped his fingers at Obadiah, who left the room immediately. "That oversight will be taken care of," Mordecai said.

"Thank you." The cop was polite and gracious. "So, why did you decide to visit our city today?"

"To celebrate Easter."

"Ah. So you'll be participating in the National Easter Service?"

"Alas, no," Mordecai said. "The council, in their misguided wisdom, refused to allow us that privilege. Now if you'll excuse me, we have to prepare for our own celebration."

"Of course, but just one more question. Do you know a man named Christian Donahue?"

"No." Mordecai looked into the officer's eyes. "Should I?"

"Not necessarily. But if you were to encounter a man named Christian Donahue, would you do me a favor? Let him know that the police would like to speak with him."

"If I were to meet him, Officer, I would certainly let him know."

"I understand. Thank you for your time." The officer put his hat back on and looked at his subordinate, and the two left.

CHAPTER FIFTY-THREE

Eddie couldn't find a parking space in the harbor area. "We're going to have to walk," he told Jamie.

"Will you be okay?" Jamie was concerned about Eddie's leg, but Eddie was already halfway down the block. Jamie, Ellen, and Peter ran to catch up. Jamie checked the time on his throwaway phone. Five thirty in the morning; the service was just an hour away.

As they approached the hotel, worshipers of all types filled the streets as they made a pilgrimage to the Pavilion. Some were dressed up in their Sunday best, others wore jeans and T-shirts, but all carried Bibles in their hands and had smiles on their faces. Jamie stopped walking when he spotted the Brethren's horse trailer on the street. A police officer was there, writing a ticket. But then Obadiah came up to the cop and started talking with him. The cop smiled and put away his ticket pad.

"Damn," Jamie said. "It looks like the police aren't going to do anything about the Brethren."

Eddie gave him a consoling pat on the back. "Well, that doesn't really surprise me. But I did hope when the police saw the Disciples, they'd run to get a warrant."

"Who are the Disciples?" Ellen asked.

Jamie was surprised by Ellen's question. "They're the Brethren's paramilitary commandos. Didn't you tell the police about them?"

"No. I just told them about the Brethren. Bible bangers. I didn't know about any paramilitary commandos, so the police aren't looking for the Delta Force type."

"Shit." Jamie brushed the hair out of his eyes and rubbed his neck. "Then the police really don't know anything. The Brethren are strange, but they don't act like murdering maniacs."

"You're right," Eddie said. "It's only when you see Mordecai with his Disciples that you realize what evil they're capable of doing."

"Then let's go to the police and tell them." Ellen grabbed Jamie's arm, but he shook it off.

"We'd be spinning our wheels. We don't have any real proof, anyway. And even if we did convince them, by the time they've called in their SWAT team, the Disciples will have started their executions."

"Then what are we supposed do?" Eddie asked.

Peter took the handgun out of his pocket. "Should we use force?"

"No." Jamie shook his head and took the gun away from him. "There are too many innocent people here."

Peter nodded and Ellen snapped her fingers. "I've got an idea. Let's go back to the van and get the ketamine. If we can administer it to the Disciples, it'll knock them out."

"Then what do we do while we're waiting for the drug to take effect? Read the Disciples a bedtime story?"

"Ketamine is supposed to work pretty fast. And while we may not be able to give a dose to everyone, we might be able to shoot up some and at least put a dent into their plans."

Jamie reluctantly agreed. When they got back to the van, Ellen took out the syringes and the vials of ketamine. She wiped her hands with a wet-nap and Jamie rolled his eyes. "Oh yeah, take extra time to be sanitary."

Ellen didn't bother looking at him. She asked Eddie to look up ketamine on her smartphone and read aloud the recommended dosages. "I'll have to guess at the Disciples' average height and weight, and hope for the best," she said as she began the process. First, she stirred the drug by rolling the vials in the palms of her hands. "I have to be careful that my movements don't make any bubbles," she said.

Then she asked Eddie to open up the syringe packages and check for any visible damage. As Eddie gave her the okay for each one, she disinfected its needle with an alcohol swab, then carefully filled each syringe to the prescribed amount and recapped the needle. "I'm guessing the average weight of the Disciples to be around a hundred and eighty pounds. Does that sound okay?"

She looked up to Jamie, but he didn't know. He nodded anyway and asked, "Then how are we going to stick it to them? So to speak."

"Unfortunately, we can't knock them out instantly. In order to do that, we'd have to administer the drug intravenously. And under these circumstances, we'd never be able to find their veins. So instead, we'll inject the ketamine intramuscularly. All you have to do is aim for a part of the leg or arm that has lots of muscle, and go for it."

"Right through their clothes?" Eddie asked.

"You want to ask them to roll up their sleeves?"

"I guess not. But how long will they be out for?" Jamie asked.

"If they're knocked unconscious, for about an hour."

Jamie was still worried. "And what if they don't go under?"

"That's a good possibility, since I don't want to kill anybody with an overdose. But even in the amounts we're giving them, they'll still be hallucinating. They won't bother us. In any event, we have to work fast."

Jamie agreed. "Is everybody ready?" They nodded, so Ellen started divvying up the syringes.

CHAPTER FIFTY-FOUR

They ran back to the hotel lobby. Jamie expected people to stare because they were wearing linen work clothes and their pant pockets bulged with syringes, but no one batted an eye.

Jamie tapped Ellen on the shoulder. "Do you know which room the Brethren are in?"

She shrugged. "No, but one of the receipts I saw was for a banquet hall."

He smiled. "Considering Mordecai has a hundred Faithfuls, a banquet hall makes sense."

They walked up to the hotel's directory. One event stood out from the rest. *Private Easter Party in the Pilgrim Hall, temporarily renamed the Son-Shine Room.*

They ran to the hall, but stopped outside the closed door. They didn't have to go in to know who was inside—Mordecai's voice wafted out through the walls. Jamie opened the door a crack to peek inside. The Brethren sat on the floor, watching Mordecai. He stood in front, dressed in white linens and a sash, with a robe over it. It looked regal with its yellow piping. On his head was a golden crown, and in his right hand he firmly grasped a huge sword. He lifted the sword above the Faithfuls and proclaimed, "God's holy servant, the Archangel Ezekiel, came to me. He told me to prepare for a disaster that will test man's faith in God."

The Faithfuls got upset, but Mordecai calmed them down.

"Do not fear. We aren't the victims of God's rage. Instead, God has appointed us to enact his will when this calamity happens."

One of the Faithfuls cried out, "What will happen?"

"In about an hour, the so-called conservative Christians will begin their Easter service. But they have angered God with their liberality. They've tainted His rules with their love of money and power. And now their very existence threatens our holy way of life. They are vile, and dirty, and spawned from the devil."

"How do we stop them?" another person asked.

"We don't have to stop them," Mordecai said. "God has appointed the Disciples to do that for us. But be warned, fulfilling God's plan will be violent. The conservative leaders must die painful deaths, and their followers will be physically and spiritually injured. That is why we've been diligently cutting gauze into bandages and assembling first aid kits."

The Faithfuls cried out in confusion, and Mordecai smiled. "God has asked us to heal the survivors' wounds. While you concentrate on their physical injuries, I'll concentrate on their spiritual maladies. The world will be so grateful that they won't call the Brethren a cult any longer. They will join the chorus of worshipers chanting 'Mordecai is great. Mordecai is good.'"

Jamie closed the door. When the Disciples began their massacre, the congregation in the Pavilion would be scared and start rioting. Then, acting like a group of Florence Nightingales, the Faithfuls would swoop in to rescue the congregation. Mordecai would become a national hero and the de facto leader of America's conservative religions.

CHAPTER FIFTY-FIVE

Jamie stopped in the lobby, and they huddled to confer. "We need to stop the Disciples first. Agreed?"

"I understand," Eddie said. "Without the Disciples, Mordecai won't be able to implement his plan. But we still don't know where the Disciples are."

Jamie wasn't deterred. "Figuring this out shouldn't be too hard. Ellen, did Chris reserve any more banquet halls?"

"I don't think so."

"Well, I counted the Disciples when they left the Brethren—there were ten of them, so they probably reserved several rooms."

"No," Peter interrupted. "They're not sleeping here. They're only getting ready for the Easter Service. Saul is too cheap. At most he'd only pay for a single suite."

"Okay, let's suppose they're all staying in one suite." Jamie nodded. "Wouldn't Mordecai make sure that the room had a special significance?" A crazy idea popped into his head. "Doesn't the Bible use numbers to symbolize things?"

Eddie rolled his eyes. "Yeah, but there are so many we don't have enough time to go through them all."

"Okay." Jamie thought for a moment. "Is there a number that symbolizes God?"

"How about the number three? The Holy Trinity."

"No, that couldn't be a room in this hotel. It's got to be at least three digits long, with the first digits being the floor number. Isn't there a number that represents the devil?"

"Yeah, in the book of Revelations there's the number of the Beast, 666."

Jamie's face lit up. "I bet that's it. Let's try that room first."

They took the elevator up to the sixth floor, and ran down the hall to find room 666. But there wasn't a room with that number.

"Okay," Jamie said, undeterred. "Let's try this again. Ellen, you talked about a verse that describes the White Horseman."

"You mean the 'conqueror bent on conquest' line? Yeah, but I have no idea where it came from."

Jamie looked at Eddie, but he didn't know, either.

Holding up her smartphone, Ellen yelled out the answer. "It's from the book of Revelations, 6:12."

"Then let's go to room 612. It's even on this floor."

"And it's a suite," Ellen said. "Chris's suite was room 1212. And since there's a suite on every floor, I'd bet room 612 is one, too."

They ran down the hallway. This time, Peter tried listening through the door, and shook his head. "I don't hear a soul."

"Damn." Jamie was finally discouraged.

In a hushed voice, Eddie said, "But it would make a lot of sense if the Disciples were quiet."

"Why do you say that?"

"Traditionally, the hours before Easter is a time to be quiet and contemplate a world without God's love."

"They're not religious, though."

"But they're preparing for a religious crime. Do you think they'd want to take any chances?"

Ellen took her syringes out of her pocket. "Does everyone have their syringes ready?"

Everyone did, so Jamie added, "There are ten Disciples and

only four of us. The math isn't in our favor. Each one of us has to inject as many Disciples as we can. Okay?"

Once again, everyone nodded. "Good. And you have your loaded handguns ready. But remember, it's last resort. The Disciples don't want to shoot us. They wouldn't want to risk getting caught before they've fulfilled their mission. But if they do shoot, they'll shoot to kill." Jamie looked around, and everyone was sufficiently worried. "Should we go knock on their door?"

"No," Ellen said. "We've got to surprise them." She ran toward a room service cart that was left in the hallway, and they followed her. Covering up the dirty dishes, she made it look like a fresh order. "Since the Disciples have never seen me before, I can pretend to be the waiter."

Jamie sighed. "But you're not dressed like a hotel employee. They'll know something's up."

"Probably," Ellen admitted. "But that'll be after I'm inside."

"You'll be in there alone, though."

"Only for a few seconds, and I'll leave the door open. I'll have a syringe tucked up each sleeve, so I'll try to inject two of them."

"What about the others?"

"Hopefully, the injected Disciples will scream, causing confusion. That will be your cue to enter."

"Okay." Jamie wasn't confident. He, Eddie, and Peter hugged the wall while Ellen approached the suite's door and gave it a knock. "Room service."

A man's voice shot out from the other side. "We didn't order anything."

"Really? It's on my ticket, sir. Suite 612, right?"

A second man shouted, "Yeah. But we told you, we didn't order anything." He opened the door and stuck his head out. "Now get the hell out of here."

Ellen didn't listen and pushed the cart inside. "Well, it would be a shame to let all this food go to waste…"

There was a brief pause. Then the first man shouted, "Fuck."

And the second man yelled, "What the hell?"

A moment later, Disciples were yelling. That was Jamie's cue. They ran into the room, syringes drawn. Jamie looked at the two men on the floor. They were in their underwear. The first was Raamiah. His eyes were open, but he had a bizarre look on his face. Jamie didn't recognize the second guy, but he was out cold. Spit dribbled down from his mouth.

Other Disciples sprinted into the room. They were in the process of getting dressed in formal military uniforms. Most didn't have weapons, but some did. Jamie handed two more syringes to Ellen, and they started injecting the enemy in the legs, the arms, the butts, or any other body part they could.

Another Disciple entered the room with a pistol in his hand. He aimed it at Eddie. Jamie spotted him and threw a plate of poached eggs in his face. While he wiped off the yellowy goo, Eddie shot him a dose.

At that moment, Raamiah started getting up and making a ruckus; he was so fat that Jamie guessed the dose wasn't large enough to put him under. "Oh my God," Raamiah said, holding each vowel as long as he could. "I'm so handsome, I'm a godsend!" He started pulling off his shirt.

"Don't worry about him," Ellen cried, injecting her third Disciple. "He's hallucinating."

"And my arms are so muscular," he continued. "I'm an Adonis."

Another Disciple approached Raamiah, attempting to help him. Peter injected him before he could do anything.

"Geez, since my arms got so big, I wonder what my private part is like." He pulled down his pants and started wailing. "Oh my God. It's gone! Somebody stole my dick!" He spotted another

Disciple and got mad. "You're the fucking thief, aren't you?" Raamiah approached the Disciple with his fists clenched. Eddie followed. As the Disciple fought off Raamiah's punches, Eddie injected him.

Raamiah turned around and looked at Eddie. "It was you!" He pulled his arm back for another punch and promptly fell to the ground.

Two more Disciples entered, their guns drawn. Peter and Ellen immediately pounced on them with their syringes.

Then Jamie heard Andy's voice. He looked up and saw the head Disciple, Sharar, grab Andy and put his gun to Andy's forehead. They were dressed in formal uniforms, and Sharar had a couple of M16s over his shoulder.

"One move, and your friend dies," Sharar shouted. He headed for the door, dragging Andy with him.

Jamie figured if Sharar shot Andy, he'd blow his chance at getting into the Easter Service unnoticed. Andy was his only remaining accomplice.

But Eddie cried out, "Please, don't…"

Sharar and Andy disappeared out the door, and Eddie began to chase them. The strain on his legs must have been too much. He fell.

Jamie did a quick head count of the disciples. "Eight down. We still have to get Andy and Sharar."

He helped Eddie off the ground, and they rushed out of the room in search of them.

CHAPTER FIFTY-SIX

Outside, the harbor looked like a carnival. The service was to begin at any minute, yet there were hundreds of people still waiting to get in. Parents held crying children in their arms and others sang Easter songs to pass the time.

Demonstrators were out in force, too. Some picketed against the council's homophobic policies. Others opposed their stance on reproductive rights. Jamie checked the area for security. He couldn't see any, or even any metal detectors at the entrances. The only thing he saw was the police department's mobile trailer parked about a half mile away. Even with its flashing red lights, it was too far away to do any good. Jamie wished he could run to the police and tell them about Sharar and the Disciples, let the police take care of everything. But he needed evidence before they would listen to him.

Jamie thought if he could point Sharar out to them, it might do the trick. He scanned the area for Sharar, but couldn't see past the crowds. But Jamie did spot Mordecai down the street, waiting. Wearing his cape and crown, he sat tall on the white horse, and his Faithfuls clamored around him. But Jamie refused to think about them. He needed to focus on preventing the massacre.

Jamie fought his way to the entrance gate and nervously stood in line for admittance. Outside the tent, a choir sang gospel songs and a large military honor guard stood at ease. It appeared that both groups were waiting for their entrance.

Ten minutes later, Jamie decided he couldn't wait any longer. He jumped over the turnstiles without a ticket, ignoring the protests of the people in front of him. Eddie, Ellen, and Peter followed and luckily, nobody stopped them. Inside, they surveyed the area. A large platform was positioned at the far end of the tent. It acted as the church sanctuary, with a large altar and a cross taking center stage.

Without notice, organ music played from the loudspeakers and a man announced, "Ladies and gentlemen, please stand for the national anthem." The congregation stood, and the choir and honor guard made their entrances. They marched to the front of the platform and the choir performed a medley of patriotic songs.

Jamie made his way to Ellen. "I don't know where Sharar and Andy are, but I see your father." He pointed to him, sitting in the front row with his so-called security men. "Let's get your father out before we do anything else."

Ellen agreed. The four snuck up behind Mr. Rhodes. They kept their guns concealed, ready if needed. "Daddy, it's me," Ellen whispered.

He turned around. "Ellen?"

"Daddy, you've got to leave." He started to argue, but Ellen cut him short. "Don't ask questions. For once, just do as I say."

He obeyed and hesitantly made his way to a side exit. The security men rose, too, but Jamie was confident they wouldn't do anything that would compromise Sharar's mission. He moved his hand to show them he was packing a weapon under his shirt. "If you even think about reaching for your guns, I'll shoot."

They didn't need any more convincing. Jamie led them out, with Eddie and Peter following them.

Outside, Ellen still argued with her father. Television satellite trucks hid the area, so Jamie felt comfortable taking the guns out of the security men's jackets. He held them up for the elder Rhodes to see, and the fighting stopped. Peter tied up the men with a couple of plastic shopping bags that he found in a

Dumpster, and Jamie handed Ellen the guns. "I think we have enough evidence to get the police involved. So why don't you and Peter escort them to the police trailer? Eddie and I will go back and find Sharar."

"Just be careful," Ellen said. She gave her prisoners a kick in the shins, and they started walking.

Jamie and Eddie went back to the Pavilion and searched for Sharar.

With a big flourish, the choir stopped singing and the honor guard finished twirling their rifles. As the groups took their places at the rear of the platform, the congregation rose, singing a rousing version of Handel's Hallelujah chorus. The ministers processed to the platform. Most of the preachers wore traditional black suits, although a few had put on colorful vestments for the occasion.

They stepped onto the front of the platform, taking center stage. But Jamie's attention stayed in the back of the platform. The number of riflemen in the honor guard looked larger than it had before. He looked at each of their faces and his heart skipped a beat. At some point, Sharar and Andy had snuck into the honor guard lineup. They wore the same uniforms and cradled identical M16s, only their rifles had real bullets.

Jamie pointed them out to Eddie. "What should we do? Storm them now, or wait for the police to come?"

Eddie shook his head. "If they see us approaching, they might start shooting. We should play it safe and stay here." Jamie agreed, and Eddie added, "But remember, we won't do anything to harm Andy."

"I know," Jamie said.

The Hallelujah chorus ended, and the congregation sat down.

CHAPTER FIFTY-SEVEN

A woman wearing a flowery dress walked up to the lectern. Zacchaeus listened to her read from the Gospel, but the message didn't comfort him. He trembled. Back in the hotel, Sharar had turned on him and made him his captive. But now Zacchaeus wasn't sure if he was still a prisoner.

When Sharar dragged him to the Pavilion, he'd asked Zacchaeus to be forgiven. "I had to pretend that I didn't love you," he told him. "I said those things to trick Jamie, so you could be saved. You understand, don't you?"

Zacchaeus told Sharar that he understood.

Sharar leaned over and whispered to him, "My little soldier, do you see them?"

Zacchaeus looked around, but nobody appeared familiar. "Whom am I supposed to see?"

"Your so-called friends, Jamie and Eddie. But they're not your friends. They want to kill you. They want to kill me, too."

Zacchaeus darted his eyes back and forth until he spotted them sitting in a pew at the back of the Pavilion. "What should we do, Disciple?"

"We need to complete our mission. You need to act like the man you are."

Zacchaeus took a breath. "As you wish, Disciple."

The woman finished her Gospel and the congregation sang

"Christ Has Risen." Zacchaeus followed Sharar's instructions to the letter. He snuck off the platform while Sharar quietly walked to the side of the Pavilion and hid behind a stage curtain.

Zacchaeus went backstage and climbed up a ladder to the lighting grid. He followed the grid's path until he was directly above the altar and had a straight line of sight to the pulpit. Nobody but Sharar knew he was there.

One of the ministers stood up for his sermon. He walked center stage with a Bible in his hand. But he didn't take his place behind the pulpit. His actions deviated from Sharar's plans. Instead, the minister delivered his words of wisdom while walking around the platform.

Zacchaeus raised his M16 and had his finger on the trigger. He followed the minister as best he could. He knew what he was about to do was wrong. He trembled and was scared. He wasn't the man Sharar thought he was. He couldn't complete the mission. He started crying and put down his rifle.

Zacchaeus looked at Sharar to say he was sorry, but Sharar angrily spat on the ground. Zacchaeus looked over at Eddie, and Eddie looked back at him. They locked eyes. Eddie stood and ran up to the altar. He shouted, "Andy, please don't do it."

The minister stopped his preaching, and the Pavilion went silent. Everyone looked at Eddie, especially Sharar, who raised his rifle, aimed it at Eddie, and prepared to fire.

Zacchaeus had to act to save his friend. He took aim at Sharar. But Sharar saw Zacchaeus's movement, changed his target, and shot him in the chest.

An explosion of pain ran through Zacchaeus's entire body. He fell from the grid, toppling onto the altar's cross. He heard the congregation scream and saw Eddie run up to him. He felt Eddie holding him, but he knew it was too late. He told Eddie that he loved him, and closed his eyes for the last time.

CHAPTER FIFTY-EIGHT

Jamie stood helpless as pandemonium swelled throughout the Pavilion. People ran to escape the shooting and ended up blocking the exits so no one could leave.

Choir members scattered in all directions. Some fell getting off the platform, and were trampled by the members behind them.

The ministers were no better. They ran for the stage door, hitting and scratching each other to get out first.

Then Mordecai entered the Pavilion riding his white stallion. In the midst of the chaos, he held his sword high and called for his Faithfuls. They came running in, armed with bandages and first aid kits.

The stallion became skittish, and Mordecai couldn't control him. The horse bucked and reared out of fear. The nearby Faithfuls were kicked and hit, falling to the ground. The stallion stomped on them as he cantered away. He only stopped when he ran into one of the tent's guylines. Mordecai fell off and cried out as the horse trampled him.

It was mayhem. Jamie forced his way to Eddie and watched him check Andy's pulse. He shook his head. He couldn't find one; he began crying. Jamie wanted to help his husband cope with the tragedy, but all he could say was, "I'm sorry."

"Thank you," Eddie replied, and gathered his composure.

"But we have work to do now." They began searching for Sharar.

They found him hiding behind the pile of broken choir risers. He looked pathetic, wearing a discarded choir robe as a disguise. Eddie grabbed him by the robe's stole and started dragging him to the police, but he didn't have to go far. The police arrived, with Christian in tow. He was handcuffed.

It took several hours and many more police officers to control the mayhem. All the news networks came out to cover the tragedy. Helicopters hovered over the harbor, taking aerial shots of the tragedy.

Jamie sat with Eddie in a corner. Ellen and Peter eventually came into the Pavilion and sat beside them. They silently watched as the police did their work.

CHAPTER FIFTY-NINE

Three Months Later

Sitting in a rental car, Jamie watched as the trees zipped past. The Catskill Mountains used to remind him of bad memories. But today he was ruled by other emotions. He looked over at Eddie, who kept his eyes fixed on the interstate. He turned to Ellen in the back. "You doing okay?"

"I'm fine, sweetcakes." She leaned forward and massaged his shoulders. "How about you?" He gave her a slight nod.

Eddie broke his silence. "We should be getting to Stratburgh soon." Jamie looked over and saw a tear running down his check. Jamie wanted to comfort him, to make all the sad feelings go away. But instead, he looked out the window. "It's too bad Peter couldn't make it."

Leaning back in her seat, Ellen said, "I hear Daddy's been keeping him pretty busy."

"Yeah," Jamie said, "I'm glad your father hired him. That was very nice."

"Trust me, Daddy didn't hire him to be nice. Daddy needed his computer knowledge."

Jamie smiled. "Yeah, not to mention his family's connections."

"Well, that, too." Ellen tapped Eddie on the shoulder. "So, how's your job search going?"

"Well, it's going," he replied. Jamie felt a jolt of remorse. As Eddie had predicted, Chef Bardot fired him for missing Easter brunch. "I hope we can continue to make ends meet."

"We'll do fine. We only have to hold out a little longer," Jamie said. "At the end of the month, I start work at Empire Investigations. I'll be a private eye. Well, an assistant to one, anyway."

Eddie exited off the tollway and onto a county road. He ignored the sign for the university and headed toward the park and the Hudson River. When they arrived, Jamie was amazed at its beauty.

"Andy always loved this area," Eddie said. "I'm glad we could do this."

Jamie nodded and put his hand on Eddie's knee. "The river is so pretty when you get north. Just looking at the water gives me a good feeling." Jamie wished he felt good today, but all he could think about was Andy's life. His sadness. In the end, Andy didn't have any family or friends. When Jamie had called Andy's father to tell him about the funeral, he refused to acknowledge he had a son.

Eddie parked by the side of the road. Getting out of the car, he straightened his tie and asked if he could carry the urn. Ellen gave it to him, and the three walked to a grassy overlook.

There were a few sailboats floating on the river below, but other than that, the park was empty. The sun shined in Jamie's eyes, but he preferred to squint rather than put on sunglasses. "Should we say anything? A prayer, maybe?"

"No," Eddie said. "I'm not sure it would be appropriate."

"Perhaps you're right." Jamie took Ellen's hand.

Eddie opened the urn and let Andy's ashes scatter down the overlook. He was crying.

Jamie tried to comfort him by saying, "You know, Andy died

a hero. If it wasn't for him, Mordecai's plan might have been successful. You might even call him a martyr."

"Maybe." Eddie wiped away his tears. "But I hope the time comes when the world doesn't need martyrs anymore."

Eddie hugged Jamie and Ellen. They started walking back to the car, but Eddie stopped them. "Can you wait a minute?"

"Sure," Jamie said. He watched Eddie go back to the overlook and cut down a couple of branches from a nearby tree. He made a cross out of the branches and planted it into the ground.

When he returned, Eddie took Jamie's hand and said, "I love you."

"I love you, too, Eddie."

Together, they walked back to the car.

About the Author

Joel Gomez-Dossi became a novelist by way of journalism, theater, television, and digital media production. He was a stage manager for several theaters in the Midwest and Southwest; a producer for television projects; and a production manager for the Emmy Award-winning PBS science series *Newton's Apple*.

Joel has written about film and theater for many regional publications across the country and penned an entertainment column for the queer press that ran in twelve states. His first novel, *Pursued*, was published in December 2012. Joel and his husband live happily ever after in upstate New York with their dog, a Treeing Walker Coonhound.